The
Rumpelstiltskin
Problem

The
Rumpelstiltskin
Problem

VIVIAN VANDE VELDE

SCHOLASTIC INC.
New York Toronto London Auckland Sydney
Mexico City New Delhi Hong Kong Buenos Aires

*This book is dedicated to hospice caregivers—
especially to those angels disguised as nurses
and volunteers at Journey Home*

ISBN 0-439-30529-2

12 11 10 9 8 7 6 5 4 3   2 3 4 5 6 7/0

Printed in the U.S.A.   40

First Scholastic printing, February 2002

The text of this book is set in 11.5-point Dante.

contents

The rumpelstiltskin problem

There's a game we used to play when I was in school that kids still play, though it has various names. We called it Gossip. Somebody would whisper something to one person, who was supposed to whisper the same thing to the next person, who whispered it to the next, and so on until the last person said it out loud, at which point everyone would laugh because little by little along the way bits and pieces had been left out or misheard, other words had been added, details were lost, the sense changed—and the final message was usually totally different from the original.

That's the way it is with fairy tales. In the beginning they were told, not written down. And over time, as the stories were repeated by different people in different situations, they constantly shifted and changed—the way *your* story might shift and change, for example, if you were caught putting shaving cream on your cat. How you justi-fied the situation to your parents might differ sharply from what you told your friends, which would probably be dif-ferent from any explanation you might offer to the cat.

That's why we sometimes have completely different versions of the same story. But in some cases, so many de-tails have been lost that the story stops making sense.

That's how I feel about the story of Rumpelstiltskin—it makes no sense.

The story starts with a poor miller telling the king, "My daughter can spin straw into gold."

We are not told how the miller has come to be talking with the king in the first place, or why the miller chooses to say such a thing. In any case, to my mind the reasonable answer for the king to come back with would be: "If your daughter can spin straw into gold, why are you a poor miller?" But the king doesn't say that; he says, "Then she shall come to my castle and spin straw into gold for me, and if she does, I'll make her my queen."

Now, no matter the reason the miller said what he did, you'd think that in reality he would have noticed that his daughter doesn't actually know how to spin straw into gold. (Unless she's lied to him. In which case you'd think that now would be the time for her to set things straight.)

But still he brings her to the castle to show off a talent he knows she doesn't have—which doesn't sound to me like responsible parenting.

At the castle the king locks the girl into a room and tells her, "Spin this straw into gold, or tomorrow you shall die."

Not my idea of a promising first date.

The girl seems smarter than her father. *She* knows that she can't spin straw into gold, so she's worried. But what does she do? She starts crying. Not a very productive plan.

Still, along comes a little man who, by happy coincidence, knows how to do what everyone wants. "What will you give me to spin this straw into gold for you?" he asks her, and she offers him her gold ring.

Now think about this.

Here's someone who can spin an entire roomful of straw into gold. Why does he need her tiny gold ring? Sounds like a bad bargain to me.

But the little man agrees and spins the straw into gold.

Is the king satisfied?

Of course not.

The next night he locks her into an even bigger room with even more straw and offers her the same deal: "Spin this straw into gold, or tomorrow you shall die."

Again the little man comes, again he gets her butt out of trouble (this time in exchange for a necklace—apparently the poor miller has a secret stash somewhere, to keep his daughter in all this jewelry), and yet again the king makes his demand: "Straw for gold."

At this point the girl has run out of jewelry, but the little man says he'll spin one more time if she'll promise him her firstborn child. Why he wants this child he never says, and she never asks. Obviously the miller's daughter is no more a responsible parent than her father is, for she agrees to the bargain.

Fortunately for everyone, the next morning the king is finally satisfied with the amount of gold the girl has spun for him, and he asks her to marry him.

Swept off her feet because he's such a sweet talker ("Spin or die"), she accepts the king's proposal.

Eventually the happy couple has a child, and the little man suddenly shows up to demand what has been promised to him.

Again the girl cries, perhaps hoping that yet another little man will step forward to get her out of trouble.

Although the deal clearly was "firstborn child for a roomful of straw spun into gold," the little man now offers the queen a way out: "Guess my name," he says, "and you may keep the child."

And if she doesn't guess his name, what does *he* get, besides the child she has already promised him? Nothing. I told you: This guy doesn't know how to bargain. You wouldn't want to go to a garage sale with him; he'd talk the prices *up*.

Now, the queen should be able to guess the little guy's name is Rumpelstiltskin by noticing that that's the name of the story, and—since nobody else in the kingdom has a name—she might go with that first. But nobody in this kingdom is very smart, so instead the queen sends the servants out into the countryside to look for likely names.

Luckily for her, at the last moment, one of the servants spots the little man dancing around a campfire singing a bad poem that ends with the line, "Rumpelstiltskin is my name." *Why* is he doing this? Because if he was singing "Kumbaya," the story would go on even longer than it already does.

Being from this kingdom of the mentally challenged, the servant doesn't recognize the importance of what he has observed. "I couldn't find any names," he tells her. "All I found was this little guy dancing around a campfire singing 'Rumpelstiltskin is my name.'" You wouldn't want to put this guy in charge of sophisticated international negotiations.

Now, we aren't told whether the queen is really, really

stupid—which would be my first choice—or whether she's playing a cruel game with the little man who, after all, three times spun gold for her and then offered her a last-minute chance to get out of her ill-chosen bargain. But when he shows up and asks if she's found out his name, she says first, "Is it George? Is it Harry?" and only then asks, "Is it Rumpelstiltskin?"

Justifiably annoyed, the little guy stamps his foot, which cracks the castle floor. (The king—who, by the way, has disappeared from the story—should have asked her to spin that straw into something useful instead of all that gold, like maybe a floor covering that wouldn't crack when a man consistently described as "little" stamped his foot.) But anyway, there's Rumpelstiltskin with his foot caught in the floor, and in a really resourceful case of well-I'll-show-them, he gets so mad he tears himself in two.

Excuse me?

What do you think your teacher would say if you handed in a story like that?

I think you'd be lucky to get a D−.

And that's assuming your spelling was good.

It was by asking myself all these questions that I came to write these stories.

I
a fairy tale in bad taste

Once upon a time, before pizzerias or Taco Bells, there was a troll named Rumpelstiltskin who began to wonder what a human baby would taste like. Now, Rumpelstiltskin had dined on sheep and snake; he had sampled catfish whiskers and spider toes; he had nibbled on vulture and on things at which vultures had turned up their noses. He had even (according to rumor) eaten troll—though no one had proof of this. But, on the other hand, no one had seen his sister-in-law Myrna in a good long time, even though the last anyone had heard of her, she was setting off to visit Rumpelstiltskin's cave. Then again, Myrna was a rather disagreeable troll, and no one had looked very hard for her.

Whatever the truth of that, suddenly Rumpelstiltskin decided that what he *really* wanted to try was human baby.

"That will be difficult to arrange," the other trolls

warned Rumpelstiltskin. "Usually human parents object to their babies being eaten."

"Besides," said Rumpelstiltskin's brother, the one who had misplaced Myrna, "babies probably just taste like chicken, anyway."

Still, Rumpelstiltskin would not be talked out of it, and he went to the St. Bartholomew's Day Faire where, it was said, you could buy anything.

But this saying proved to be wrong: Rumpelstiltskin could not find a single merchant selling baby. The closest he came was a woman who countered by volunteering to sell him her teenager, but even then Rumpelstiltskin doubted it was an entirely serious offer.

Well, Rumpelstiltskin said to himself, *if I cannot BUY a baby for lunch, perhaps I can STEAL one.*

But he had no better luck at this than at the other. He stood very, very still so that he looked—as most trolls will—like a huge harmless rock as he waited patiently in the middle of the fairgrounds. Even so, nobody left a baby untended near him. The younger a human baby was, the more its parents seemed to be careful of it, and Rumpelstiltskin was determined to have a very young human baby so that its flesh would be tender and sweet.

Finally, Rumpelstiltskin said to himself, *Well, I cannot buy a baby, and I cannot steal one. Maybe I can get one by trick-*

ery. So he continued to stand very still and quiet and he watched the humans and listened to their talk, until finally a plan came to him. It wasn't the best plan, because it required a lot of waiting, but trolls generally live for hundreds of years, so they tend to be patient.

Rumpelstiltskin had been watching a miller and his daughter who looked a little bit shabby—though they were both clean—and who seemed gullible. Rumpelstiltskin tried to rearrange the crags of his face into a friendly expression, then he went up to them, moving like a mountain to a prophet, and said, "I know how you can earn a coin or two. Do you see the king sitting there in his royal carriage enjoying the street performers? I have been watching him throw coins to the puppeteers and the jugglers. I'm certain if you could make him laugh, he would throw a gold coin your way, too."

"But I don't juggle," the miller said. "And I have no puppets."

"But you could tell him a joke," Rumpelstiltskin suggested.

"If I knew a good one," the miller agreed, trying to think of a funny story.

"How about," the daughter started, "the one about the chicken? No, wait, it was a hedgehog—wasn't it?—and it was going . . . Where was it going now? I think . . ."

This was going to be even easier than Rumpelstiltskin had thought. "I know what would make the king laugh," he told the miller. "Tell him your daughter can spin straw into gold."

The miller and his daughter looked at each other.

"That's not *terribly* funny," the miller pointed out.

"The king has a very well-developed sense of humor," Rumpelstiltskin assured them. "Let me go before you to prepare the way."

Rumpelstiltskin made his way through the crowd like a rolling boulder until he came up to the window of the king's carriage. "Sire," Rumpelstiltskin said, bowing low like a small mountain collapsing, "I have a very sad story to tell you about a desperate man and his poor daughter."

The king, who was young and softhearted, looked where Rumpelstiltskin pointed: to the miller and his daughter, waving shyly.

"Those people," Rumpelstiltskin said, "have no money at all. They haven't eaten in days. But they are too proud to accept charity. And now the father's wits are addled from hunger, and he is going around telling people his daughter can spin straw into gold. It's enough to break a troll's heart."

Actually, there's very little that can break a troll's heart, but the king didn't know this and so he said, "That *is* sad. What can be done?"

"Perhaps," Rumpelstiltskin said, "you could pay the father to let the girl come spin straw into gold for you. Then he would have money to buy food for himself and the rest of his family. And, with the girl in your palace, you could see to it that she had a decent meal or two before you sent her home. The whole thing hinges on making them believe that you believe their story."

"That's a fine idea," said the king. "What a clever troll you are!"

So, smiling—with his lips closed, of course, so no one would notice his sharp, pointed teeth—Rumpelstiltskin waved for the miller and his daughter to join them.

"Hello," the miller said to the king. "This is my daughter, Siobhan, and she can spin straw into gold."

"Excellent!" the king declared jovially. "Wonderful!" He handed the miller a gold coin.

"Thank you," the miller said, bowing and laughing, amazed that the troll's joke worked so well after all. The girl laughed, too, and curtsied.

"Siobhan shall come to my palace and spin gold for me," the king said.

"Ho, ho!" the miller chortled. "That's a good one, Your Highness."

The king motioned for his servants to help Siobhan up into the royal carriage.

Siobhan hesitated, and her father's smile wavered. Behind the servants, Rumpelstiltskin touched his gnarled fingers to the corners of his mouth, indicating for them to continue to smile.

"I'll return her to you in a day or two," the king said, "after she's finished spinning."

"The king certainly knows how to tell them," Rumpelstiltskin whispered encouragingly to the miller and his daughter.

The miller laughed again, though not quite so heartily, and Siobhan let herself be helped into the carriage.

The king motioned the driver to start, and the horses began moving the carriage down the street.

The miller waved until the carriage turned the corner, at which time he stopped waving, stopped smiling, and said, "But . . . But . . ."

Rumpelstiltskin stepped back into the crowd and silently slipped away, like a mountain pretending to be part of the festivities.

◆　◆　◆

That night, Rumpelstiltskin climbed the wall of the king's palace and entered the room that had been set aside for Siobhan. "Hello," Rumpelstiltskin said in his gravelly voice, looking approvingly at all the straw that the king had provided for her to spin.

Siobhan was wearing a beautiful gown that the king had given her, since she was his guest. She was sprawled on the bed with her hands over her stomach and she said, "That was the biggest and best meal I ever had."

"Well, that's nice," Rumpelstiltskin said. "There's nothing like dying on a full stomach."

"*Dining* on a full stomach?" Siobhan asked.

"Dying," Rumpelstiltskin repeated.

Siobhan sat up hurriedly. "What do you mean?"

Rumpelstiltskin put on a sad face. "I just heard the king give orders," he lied, "that if you fail to spin this straw into gold by morning, your head is to be chopped off."

"*What?*" Siobhan squeaked. "Is this part of the joke?"

Rumpelstiltskin shook his head solemnly. "Apparently," he said, "the king doesn't have as good a sense of humor as I thought."

"What am I going to do?" Siobhan asked.

"Start spinning straw into gold," Rumpelstiltskin recommended.

"But I don't know how."

"Well," Rumpelstiltskin said, "maybe you can find someone who does."

"Fat chance," Siobhan said. "Between now and dawn?"

"Well," Rumpelstiltskin said again, "actually, by chance, *I* know how to spin straw into gold."

"That would be very appropriate," Siobhan pointed out, "seeing as how you're the one who got me into this mess."

That was, in fact, a very good point, but Rumpelstiltskin ignored it. "What would you give me for doing this for you?"

Siobhan looked at him in disbelief. "What could I possibly give someone who can spin straw into gold? What could such a person—or troll—possibly want?"

Rumpelstiltskin decided to start off slowly and not show his true culinary intentions. "How about if you give me that gold buckle from your gown's belt?"

Siobhan looked from the belt to Rumpelstiltskin to the straw to Rumpelstiltskin. "Are you sure this isn't part of the joke still?" she asked suspiciously.

Rumpelstiltskin held his hand out and Siobhan gave him the buckle. He pulled a stool up to the spinning wheel and began to spin. All night long he spun, until by morning there was no straw left, only piles of gauzy gold.

"Well, thank you," Siobhan said. "I'm sure the king is likely to be pleased."

In fact, the king was ecstatic. Rumpelstiltskin, lurking about the corners of the palace later that morning, heard his cries of amazement and delight.

That night, Rumpelstiltskin once more went to Siobhan's room. Actually, it was a bigger, finer room, and she was wearing an even richer and more elegant gown than the one the king had given her the day before. "So, he liked the gold?" Rumpelstiltskin asked Siobhan, without even greeting her.

"Very much," Siobhan said. "He said he never suspected I could spin *so much* straw into gold. I think he's rather too trusting for a king, but he *is* cute. He gave me a great hug and called me a treasure."

"Well, no wonder," Rumpelstiltskin said. "He hopes you'll provide him with endless treasure."

"No, I don't think that's it," Siobhan started to say, but Rumpelstiltskin interrupted her, saying, "Because I heard him say: 'Let her spin this second roomful of straw into gold, or tomorrow she shall be stoned to death.'"

"That doesn't sound like him at all," Siobhan said.

"But there *is* all this straw in here," Rumpelstiltskin pointed out.

Siobhan bit her lip anxiously.

"I'll tell you what," Rumpelstiltskin said. "Give me the clasp that holds the collar of your gown, and I will spin *this* straw into gold also."

"This gold clasp?" Siobhan asked doubtfully, fingering the exquisite but tiny object.

"That very one," Rumpelstiltskin said, for he had something much, much more valuable and tasty on his mind.

Siobhan unfastened the clasp and once more watched Rumpelstiltskin work to make straw into gold. "You're too kind," she murmured when he had finished.

"Not at all," Rumpelstiltskin answered.

And he meant it.

That night, he found her in a luxurious room, and she was wearing a gown that was made of gold cloth woven from the gold that he had spun from straw.

Hardly able to hide his glee, Rumpelstiltskin said, "I hear the king has said you must spin this new roomful of straw into gold or he will burn you at the stake."

"I think you must have heard wrong," Siobhan said. "If the king was *that* greedy, he would never have given me this dress. I'm sure he's pleased enough with the gold. In fact, he is a kind and gentle man, and we have spent the last days talking and getting to know each other, and he has asked me to marry him." She smiled in pleasure and shyly added, "And I have said yes."

"Well, congratulations," Rumpelstiltskin said. His plan was so close to completion that he could practically *taste* that baby. He said, "But why shouldn't the king give you a dress of gold, when he thinks you can spin him all the gold he could ever need? And as far as not burning you at the stake, look out the window."

Siobhan looked. Her eyes widened with horror when she saw that there was a stake in the ground right below her window, with bundles of sticks strewn about it, and she had no way of knowing that it was Rumpelstiltskin who had set that stake up to look as though the king was preparing for an execution.

"What will you give me," Rumpelstiltskin asked, "to spin this roomful of straw into gold for you?"

"I can give you this whole dress," Siobhan said, "if you give me a chance to change into one of the others the king has given me."

"Why would I want your dress?" Rumpelstiltskin sneered.

"It has much more gold to it than the belt buckle or the clasp I gave you before," Siobhan pointed out.

Rumpelstiltskin shrugged his rocky shoulders. "I have enough gold."

"I would have thought you had enough gold before," Siobhan said. "How about this ruby necklace the king gave me?"

Rumpelstiltskin shook his head.

"Or this diamond engagement ring?"

Again Rumpelstiltskin shook his head.

"Well, then, what?"

Rumpelstiltskin stroked his chin, which had warts like pebbles. Slowly, as though he couldn't make up his mind, he said, "I don't know . . ." while—all the while—all he wanted was to shout: YOUR BABY! I WANT TO EAT YOUR FIRSTBORN BABY! Instead, he said, "I'll spin the straw for you tonight, and let you know later what you must pay me."

Siobhan sighed and said, "All right," and sat down on the floor by the spinning wheel.

Foolish human! Rumpelstiltskin thought. He smacked his lips and set to work spinning.

By dawn, Rumpelstiltskin had spun this third room full of straw into gold, but he did not tell Siobhan what its cost would be.

That day, the king announced his betrothal to Siobhan, and still Rumpelstiltskin did not step forward to declare what Siobhan owed him.

Apparently Siobhan was much cleverer than Rumpelstiltskin had first thought, and had been paying much better attention than he had ever suspected while he spun, for in the coming days she began to spin straw into gold on her own, and *still* Rumpelstiltskin waited.

The marriage took place, and time passed, and it was announced that the queen was with child, and *even then* Rumpelstiltskin did not reveal himself.

He waited until the child was born: a prince, an heir to the kingdom. And then—only then—did Rumpelstiltskin go to the queen.

"Remember that you have not paid me for that last roomful of gold?" he said to her as she rocked the tiny baby. *Scrumptious,* Rumpelstiltskin thought. *That baby smells scrumptious.*

"Of course," Siobhan said with a generous smile. "Have you made up your mind, then?"

"I want the baby," Rumpelstiltskin announced.

Siobhan stopped rocking. She looked into his eyes and knew to not even ask if he was joking. "Take me instead," she offered.

"I don't want you," Rumpelstiltskin said. "I want baby rump roast."

Siobhan shuddered, but did not cry or beg. "You took

all the hours of the night to spin the straw into gold," she said. "Therefore you owe me all the hours of this day before I give you the child."

One day wouldn't toughen the meat, Rumpelstiltskin decided, so—generously, he thought—he agreed.

He wasn't, however, generous enough to give a moment beyond sunset, and he was back at the palace the instant the sun dipped below the horizon. This time, the king was in the room with Siobhan and the baby. Rumpelstiltskin sniffed the air, to see if there might be soldiers hiding behind the tapestries that hung on the walls. There was a strong scent of troll, which told Rumpelstiltskin that it was time for his yearly bath, but he could smell no other humans in the room, just the scent of the king, Queen Siobhan, and the sweet, enticing, delicious aroma of baby.

Rumpelstiltskin finished tying his bib around his neck and said, "Hand it over."

"How about," the king suggested smoothly, "a deal?"

"Don't want you, don't want your missus," Rumpelstiltskin said, "just hand the baby chops over."

But the king said something intriguing. He said, "Double or nothing?"

"Beg pardon?" Rumpelstiltskin asked.

The king and his queen exchanged a nervous look, but

the king said in a steady voice, "We propose a riddle. If we guess your name, you go away and leave us alone and promise never to bother another human family. If we don't guess your name, you get to have our second-born child as well as our firstborn."

Rumpelstiltskin was so excited, he was practically drooling. He couldn't lose. First of all, there was no way these two humans could ever know his name. Second of all, even if somehow they managed to *guess* correctly, all he had to do was claim they had gotten it wrong. So he said, "All right. Guess away."

Siobhan closed her eyes in what could have been relief or dismay, but when she opened them what she said, calmly and clearly, was, "Is your name Rumpelstiltskin?"

Now how in the world had they ever guessed that? Rumpelstiltskin wondered. But trolls' skin is rocky, so his expression never changed as he said, "Wrong. Too bad. Hand over the kiddie cutlets."

But even as he put his scaly arms out to take the baby, another scaly arm pulled back one of the tapestries, and out stepped—of all trolls—his own brother. "Your name is too Rumpelstiltskin," his brother said. "You've lost the riddle. No human baby for you now or ever."

Rumpelstiltskin felt as though he'd had dinner yanked from his very mouth. He could feel his taste buds quiver.

He stamped his foot and howled, "What are you doing? What's the matter with you? I want that baby!" He stamped his foot again, and a thin crack appeared on the tiles, for trolls, being creatures of the earth, are very powerful.

"Don't you be pulling any of your nonsense with me," his brother warned, shaking a boulder-like finger at him. "I went into your cave looking for you, and I found one of my Myrna's ears under your dining room table."

"Coincidence!" Rumpelstiltskin protested and stamped his foot again. The crack burst open, miles deep from the strength of a troll's rage, and Rumpelstiltskin tipped head over heels into the hole he himself had made.

His brother, perhaps feeling some last twinge of family loyalty despite the unfortunate incident with Myrna, grabbed for him. Rumpelstiltskin dangled for a long, long moment.

But then his leg broke off in his brother's stony grip and Rumpelstiltskin continued to fall down, down, down with a howl that took a long time to fade away.

"Oops!" his brother said. He turned and saw that the king was fanning his wife, who—though she kept a strong grip on the baby—looked close to fainting. Rumpelstiltskin's brother wondered if this had anything to do with the leg he was still holding.

So he ate it.

II

stɾɑw inꞇo gold

Once upon a time, in the days before Social Security or insurance companies, there lived a miller and his daughter, Della, who were fairly well-off and reasonably happy until the day their mill burned down.

Suddenly they had nothing except the clothes they were wearing: no money, nor any way to make money, nor any possibility of ever getting money again unless they came up with a plan.

Now the miller was very good at milling, and he was fairly good at being a father, but at planning he was no good at all.

His plan was this: They would sit by the side of the road and wait for someone who looked rich to pass by. Then the miller would announce: "My daughter can spin straw into gold. If you give us three gold pieces, she will spin a whole barnful of straw into gold for you." If the rich people were interested—and the miller pointed out that they couldn't help but be interested—he would then say that his daughter's magic only worked by moonlight. "You must leave her alone—completely undisturbed—all night long. And by dawn all of the straw will be spun into gold."

"I don't understand this plan," Della said. "I'm not very good at spinning, even wool, and I have no idea how—"

"No, no," the miller interrupted, "you don't understand."

"That's what I just said." Della sighed.

"Listen," the miller explained, "the plan, of course, is for the two of us to take our fee of three gold pieces and run away during the night."

"That's dishonest," Della pointed out.

"So it is," her father admitted. "But we will take those three gold pieces and rebuild our mill. Once the mill is working again, we will save all our money until we can repay the people we've tricked."

Della still didn't like this plan, but since she herself had no experience beyond milling and being a daughter, she agreed.

So Della and her father sat by the side of the road, and the first rich person to pass by was the richest person in the land: he was the king.

"Oh, dear," Della said, recognizing the royal crest on the door of the carriage, "maybe we should wait—"

But if the miller was not good at making plans, he was even worse at changing plans once they were made. Standing in the middle of the road, he called out, "My daughter can spin straw into gold. If you give us three gold pieces, she will spin a whole barnful of straw into gold for you."

The king motioned for the driver to stop the horses. "You," he said, leaning out of the window. "Both of you, come closer." The king had clothes of red satin and brocade, sewn with gold thread. He wore more rings than he had fingers, and he had a dark wig, which was all thick ringlets around his pale face. He put a silk handkerchief to his nose, for Della and her father still smelled of smoke from their burned-down mill. "What did you say?" he demanded.

The miller wasn't sure if this question meant the king was interested and he should now explain about the moonlight and the being left alone, or if it meant the king was slightly deaf and hadn't heard the first part. The miller decided he'd better repeat himself. He raised his voice and enunciated clearly. "My daughter can spin straw into gold. If you give us three gold pieces, she will spin a whole barnful of straw into gold for you."

"If she can spin straw into gold," the king asked, "then why are the two of you dressed in filthy rags?"

"Ah," the miller said. "Well . . ." Once again he had been all prepared to explain about the moonlight and the being left alone, and now that he couldn't say that, he had no idea what to say. "Why are we dressed in rags?" he repeated. "That's a very good question. That's an excellent question."

The king dabbed at his nose, then let his handkerchief drop into the mud by the road, since he only ever used a handkerchief once. He pulled out a new one.

"Our mill burned down," Della explained.

"Yes," the miller agreed. "Including the spinning wheel. And the straw."

"Hmmm," the king said. "Very well. You may follow the carriage to the castle. You will be provided with your three gold pieces, a spinning wheel, and straw." He dropped his second handkerchief without having used it at all and motioned for the driver to get the horses moving.

The miller nudged his daughter as they started down the road after the carriage. "See," he said. "I told you the plan would work."

"Yes," Della said, "so you did." But she was still worried.

And rightly so. For when they got to the castle, the plan began to fall apart.

The king insisted that Della work at her spinning in the castle itself instead of in the barn.

"But," the miller protested, "she needs to work her magic at night, by the light of the moon."

"Fine," the king said. "The rooms on the second floor have windows to let in the moonlight."

The miller gulped, since it would be harder to get Della away if she was up on the second floor. He tried again. "But if anybody interrupts Della while she's working her magic, the magic will reverse itself and all the gold she's spun will turn back into straw."

"We'll lock her in the room to make sure nobody interrupts her," the king said.

Della gave her father a warning nudge before he could say anything else to make matters even worse.

"And of course," the king said, "if she fails to spin this straw into gold, I will have her head chopped off." To the servants he said, "Lock this man away for the night so he doesn't try to escape." As two of the largest servants took the miller by the arms, the king told him, "Come back tomorrow, and I will give you your three gold pieces or your daughter's head."

"But . . . but . . ." the miller started, but before he could think of anything to say, he was dragged out of the room.

Leaving Della, for the first time in her life, on her own.

The king had her led up to a room that was as big as the entire mill had been. Servants brought in a spinning wheel, and then load after load after load after load of straw until the whole room was filled with straw, except for the area around the spinning wheel.

How am I ever going to get out of this? Della thought. She hoped to slip out of the room while the servants were making their deliveries, but someone was always watching her. Then, after the king's guards locked her in, she tried to get the door open with her hairpin, the way heroines in stories always do, but in the end all she had was a bent hairpin. She couldn't even climb out the window, which was too narrow to pass through and very high up. And even if she did get out—what about her father?

She kicked the spinning wheel, which made her feel a little bit better but not much.

The servants hadn't even given her anything to eat, and now as the room got darker and darker until the only light was the moonlight coming through her prison window, Della added dinner to the list of meals she'd missed that day.

Sitting on the hard floor, the last thing in the world she intended to do was to start crying, but that's exactly what she did.

After a while—after a long while—she used her sleeve to rub her eyes and nose, since she didn't have a handkerchief, silk or otherwise. From behind her came the sound of someone clearing his throat discreetly. Out of the corner of her eye, Della saw that whoever was behind her was offering her a handkerchief.

Without turning around, Della tried to work out exactly what she would say. "You see," she started, "actually crying is necessary for the magic . . . Tears, tears are the lubricant for the spinning wheel . . . but it only works if I'm totally alone, and since you were watching, I won't be able to do the spell again until—" At this point, she did turn around, and she stopped talking midexplanation.

She'd been expecting to see the king or one of his servants. Instead, crouched beside her was a young man who was obviously not even human. In fact, he was an elf. Tall and slender, with pointy ears, he'd been listening very attentively, if somewhat quizzically.

"Well, that doesn't make a lot of sense," he told her, but then he smiled, and she saw that he was handsome in a strange, otherworldly way. He added, "But I do admire your quick thinking."

"Who are you?" Della gasped in surprise. "What do you want? How did you get in here?"

The young elf paused a moment to consider, then answered in the order she'd asked: "Rumpelstiltskin. I heard you crying and came to see what was the matter. Sideways between the particles."

"What?" Della asked.

The elf raised his voice slightly. "Rumpelstiltskin. I heard you crying and—"

"No," Della said, "I mean . . . *sideways?*"

Rumpelstiltskin nodded. "The world of humans and the world of magic exist side by side." He illustrated by holding his hands out, his long, slender fingers spread, then he put his hands together, intertwining his fingers. "So that we're taking up the space that you're not"— he was watching her skeptically as if suspecting that she wasn't getting this, which she wasn't— "and vice versa."

"Oh," she said. "And you heard me crying from your world?"

"Well," the young elf said gently, "you were crying quite loudly."

Della finally took the handkerchief he was offering and wiped her nose. Blowing would have been more effective, she knew, but too noisy and undignified. "I don't usually cry. I know it's stupid and it doesn't help anything and it's unattractive and—"

"And I heard it," Rumpelstiltskin said. "And I came to

see what was the matter. So sometimes it *does* help." He stood and looked around the room. "Castle," he said as though he hadn't noticed before where he was. "Despite the straw." He looked more closely at Della. "You don't look like a castle person."

"I'm not," she admitted. "I'm a mill person. Except that our mill burned down. And my father told the king I could spin straw into gold so that we could get a little bit of gold from the king so that we could rebuild the mill and then we would have paid the gold back except that the king locked my father in the dungeon and me in here and I have to spin all this straw into gold tonight or he's going to cut off my head."

Rumpelstiltskin was obviously impressed. "You can spin straw into gold?"

"No," Della said.

"Then," Rumpelstiltskin said, "I think your plan has a flaw."

"That's why I was crying." Della rested her face in her hands.

"You're not going to start crying again, are you?" Rumpelstiltskin asked, sounding worried.

"No," Della said. "You can go back where you came from. I won't bother you again."

But the young elf stayed where he was.

After a while he said, "You weren't *bothering* me. I just wish I could help you."

The sad thing was that, even without raising her head and looking at him, Della could tell he was sincere. Helpless, but sincere.

"I think it's really sweet," he continued, "that you were planning to return the money even before the king gave it to you. But I've never heard of spinning straw into gold. I wouldn't know where to begin."

"That's all right," Della said. "Probably getting one's head chopped off is less unpleasant than starving to death."

After another while Rumpelstiltskin said, "But I do have another idea."

Della finally looked up.

"We could throw the straw out the window, then I could replace it with gold from my world, so long as it doesn't have to be spun out."

"I'm sure the king wouldn't complain no matter what form the gold was in, but would you really be willing to do that?"

Rumpelstiltskin nodded. "In exchange."

"In exchange for what?" Della asked.

"What do you have?"

Della considered. The mill had burned down. All she had was what she'd been wearing when the fire had started: her second-best dress with her mother's wedding ring pinned to the collar for decoration. "I have this gold ring, which belonged to my mother before she died," Della said, unpinning the ring and holding it out.

Rumpelstiltskin looked from her to the ring and back to her again. "You want me to substitute this straw for a roomful of gold, and you're offering me one gold ring in exchange?"

Della felt her face go red in embarrassment. "I'm sorry," she said. "I wasn't thinking—"

"No, no," Rumpelstiltskin said. "I didn't mean . . ." She could tell he was genuinely distressed he'd embarrassed her. "The ring will be fine."

She handed it over, for even if he meant to take it and run and never come back with gold for the straw, she wouldn't be any worse off than she was now.

But he didn't run off. He kept disappearing (sideways, he insisted, between the particles), but he kept returning with gold cups and gold coins and gold jewelry, assuring her that everything would be fine, that the king couldn't possibly chop off her head. And Della kept throwing straw out the window, till the next thing she knew, she heard the king's voice on the other side of the door saying, "It's dawn. Unlock the door." She threw the last armful of straw out the window, and when she turned back, Rumpelstiltskin was gone and the king was standing in the doorway, blinking in amazement.

"Well done," the king said, taking a bit of snuff. "I must say: well done."

"Thank you sir," Della said, curtsying. "Now if you don't mind, sir . . ."

Before she could finish, the king gestured to one of the pages, who reached into a bag hanging from his belt. He picked out three gold coins and dropped them, one by one, into Della's hand.

"Thank you, sir," Della said, curtsying again. "I—"

"In fact," the king said, "this is so well done, I think we'll hire you again for tonight."

"Oh," Della said, "but—"

The king gestured to another page. "Clean her up," he ordered. "Feed her. Keep her amused till tonight." He looked around the room appreciatively again. "Well done," he repeated.

Which didn't make Della feel any better at all.

The servants dressed Della in a gown richer than any she'd ever had. And they laid out a banquet for her, the most delicious food she'd ever tasted, on silver dishes. And all day long different ones played the lute and sang songs for her, and they brushed her hair till it shone like silk, and they manicured her nails and were friendly in every way. But when evening came, they locked her in a room even bigger than the first and filled, except for the area around the spinning wheel, with straw.

Della sat down on the floor. *Well,* she told herself, *except for the threat of getting your head chopped off, you've never had a more wonderful day.* Then she tried to tell herself that she was lucky to have had the day, but she didn't feel lucky. All that gold Rumpelstiltskin had brought, and here she was back where she had started. It was kind of him to have tried to help, but it was all for nothing. She put her face in her hands and sighed.

And looked up again when she felt a gentle touch on her arm. "I wasn't crying," she pointed out.

"No," Rumpelstiltskin said, "but this time I was looking for you." He walked around the room, or at least that part of the room that wasn't filled with straw. "More straw into gold," he observed. "Is the king still threatening to cut off your head?"

Della nodded.

"Did he even pay you for the last batch?"

Della held out the three gold coins the king's page had given her.

"Quite a bargain." Rumpelstiltskin crouched down beside her. "Offer them to me, and I'll bring more gold."

"Offer you three gold coins for a roomful of gold?" Della said. "At least the ring had sentimental value."

Rumpelstiltskin just smiled at her. "Offer them to me," he repeated.

Della put the gold coins into his hand.

Then, just as they had done the previous night, Rumpelstiltskin brought armloads of gold from between the particles while Della threw straw out the window. But this time Della knew the king would be pleased, so, instead of worrying, she and Rumpelstiltskin talked and laughed together as though they were old friends.

By the time the king returned at dawn, all the straw was gone and the room was filled with gold.

"Thank you," Della whispered as they heard the key turn in the lock.

Rumpelstiltskin bowed, then disappeared.

The door banged open.

"Well done!" the king exclaimed once again. "Truly, magnificently well done."

"Yes," Della said. "And now I must be leaving or my father will be wor—"

"Nonsense," the king said. "Your father is fine. And we're having such a good time together. I insist you stay."

"*Stay?*" Della repeated.

"Of course," the king said. "Someone with your abilities will make an excellent queen."

"*Queen?*" Della repeated.

The king gave a gracious nod. "Spin another roomful of straw into gold, and we'll consider it your dowry. I'll marry you the following day."

"Oh my," Della said.

The king gestured to one of the servants. "Dress her in the finest silks and jewels," he ordered. "Feed her off my own dishes. Treat her like a queen till tonight."

"But," Della started, "but—"

The king kissed her hand and swept out of the room.

The servants dressed Della in a gown richer than any she'd ever seen, heavy with beads and jewels, and there were more jewels for around her neck and fingers and to hang from her ears; and they laid out a banquet for her, with food even more sumptuous than the day before, and they served it on dishes of ivory, with knives and spoons of gold; and all day long they played violins and harpsichords for her; and they brushed her hair till it shone like gold, and pedicured her nails, and were respectful in every way. But when evening came, they locked her in a room even bigger than the first two rooms and filled, except for the area around the spinning wheel, with straw.

"Rumpelstiltskin," Della said out loud, "if ever there was a time I needed you, now is it."

The young elf appeared before her. He bowed just as he'd been bowing when he'd disappeared that morning, as though he'd been waiting all day to come back to her.

"This time," Della said, "at least I have something to offer you." Taking off the ruby earrings, she said, "And I've thought of a way out of this: I'll tell the king that my magic spinning cannot be done more than three times for any one person. Three is a magical number, you know." She unfastened the diamond necklace, but Rumpelstiltskin hadn't even taken the earrings yet. "What's the matter?" she asked.

"Those aren't yours to give," he said. "Those are the king's."

"Oh." Della indicated her rings, and the jewels sewn into the bodice of her dress.

Rumpelstiltskin shook his head. "Didn't the king pay you for the second roomful of gold?"

"No," Della said. "He told me he would marry me and make me queen."

"I see," Rumpelstiltskin said. "First he says, 'Spin the

straw into gold, or I'll chop your head off,' then he says, 'Spin the straw into gold, or I'll chop your head off,' and then he says, 'Spin the straw into gold, and I'll marry you.' The man has a way with words. No wonder you want to marry him."

"That's not fair," Della protested. "It's not every day a miller's daughter gets the chance to marry a king."

"No," Rumpelstiltskin said softly. "I would imagine not."

Della shivered. Having come so far, she had finally let herself think that she might actually survive her father's plan. She said, "I have nothing to offer you."

Rumpelstiltskin looked at her for a long moment before answering. "Then," he said, "I will do it for you for nothing."

Once again they worked together, Rumpelstiltskin bringing gold from his world into the locked room while Della threw straw out the window. But while the first night they had worked frantically, unsure whether the king would be fooled, and while the second night they had worked enjoying each other's company—this third night they had nothing to say to each other, and they worked silently and grimly.

As Della threw the last handfuls of straw out the window, she turned to the young elf who had three times now saved her life and said, "Rumpelstiltskin, I—"

But he had already returned to his own world without a word, leaving Della to wait for the king alone in the graying dawn.

The king was delighted with his new roomful of gold, but when Della told him that the laws of magic prohibited her from spinning any more gold for him, he complained bitterly that she had tricked him. He was all for chopping her head off, but the king's advisors said that, since the royal marriage had already been announced, this would probably be a bad idea.

And so the king and the miller's daughter were married.

The king decreed that, as queen, Della was prohibited from doing common things such as spinning, and he used this as an excuse for why she no longer spun straw into gold. And as for the miller, the king pronounced him Master Miller of the Realm, and all the other millers had to pay a tax to support him so that the king's father-in-law wouldn't have to support himself by common labor either.

But the king begrudged the gold Della no longer spun, and the marriage was not a happy one.

Eventually Della announced that she was expecting a child. This made the king happy, for he said it was time he had an heir. But when the child was born, it was a girl, and the king, saying a girl did not make a fit heir, wouldn't even visit his new daughter.

"Name her what you will," the king told Della. "It's no concern of mine."

Della sat on the window ledge of the nursery and rocked her unnamed baby daughter back and forth, so furious her eyes filled with angry tears. She stared out the window, so that her tears wouldn't fall on the infant, for she was determined that the child should never learn how her own father did not love her.

From beside her, a soft voice said, "She's lovely," and Della turned and saw Rumpelstiltskin gently touch the baby's tiny hand. "She's lovely," Rumpelstiltskin repeated. "She looks just like you. Why are you crying?"

It was the first time Della had seen him in over a year, since that last morning in that room full of gold. She wanted to tell him how very pleased she was to see him, how she had thought of his kindness every day of her queenship, but instead she blurted out how the king was disappointed to have a daughter instead of a son.

"Anyone with any sense would be proud to have her as

a daughter," Rumpelstiltskin said. "But maybe you could tell the king that when she gets to be older she'll be able to spin straw into gold." He knelt beside her. "I'll come back," he promised, "and bring him three more roomsful."

"That's very kind of you," Della said. "But I'm sure he'd love her if he only stopped to think about it."

In a very quiet voice Rumpelstiltskin said, "I don't think love is something you stop to think about."

"What I mean is," Della said, "I'm sure he *does* love her, but he just doesn't realize it. Maybe I should tell him she's sick. If he's worried about her, then he'll see how precious she is."

"But the servants would tell him she isn't sick," Rumpelstiltskin pointed out. "You could tell him a wicked old elf is going to steal her away unless . . ."

Rumpelstiltskin paused to consider, and Della said, "You don't look wicked or old."

Rumpelstiltskin smiled at her, which made him look even less wicked and old.

It almost made Della wish . . . But that was too dangerous a thought.

"We'll tell him that you're the one who taught me how to spin straw into gold," she said. "And that in exchange I promised you my firstborn child. The only way to break the agreement . . ." She sighed. "Whatever you ask the king to do," she said, "it has to be something easy, to make sure he can do it."

"Certainly," Rumpelstiltskin agreed. "How easy?"

Della thought and finally said, "He has to guess your name."

"Easier," Rumpelstiltskin suggested. "It's not that common a name."

"Tell him you'll give him three days before you'll take the baby," Della said. "Surely in that time we can arrange some way for somebody to learn your name."

But it wasn't as easy as Della thought.

The king was too busy with councils and court decisions to even ask why a wicked old elf wanted his daughter. But he did have the servants in the castle write out a list of all the names they could think of.

The next day, when Rumpelstiltskin appeared in the throne room, the king read out every name they had, starting with Aaron and ending with Zachary.

Rumpelstiltskin shook his head after each name, and when it was over he said they had two more days but they'd never guess.

The king had to be at the dedication of a new ship that

day, but he ordered the councillors and scholars of the castle to look through all the old history chronicles and put together a list of every name they could find.

The next day, Rumpelstiltskin again appeared in the throne room, and the king read out this new list, starting with Absalom and ending with Ziv.

Once again Rumpelstiltskin shook his head after each name, but this time he gave Della a worried look before announcing they had one more day but they'd never guess. He was beginning to worry, Della could tell, that they never would.

The king had been invited to a hunting party with the neighboring king, but before leaving he sent servants out of the castle into the countryside to see if they could discover any new names.

As the servants trickled back home that night and the next morning, one after another with no new names, Della decided that she would have to just blurt out the name Rumpelstiltskin and hope that the king didn't ask where she'd heard it.

Then the last of the castle servants returned.

"Good news, Your Majesty," this last man said to her. "Although I searched all day yesterday without finding any new names, as I was walking through the woods on the way back to the castle this morning, I came across that same elf who's been threatening the young princess. Fortunately he didn't see me. And even more fortunately he was dancing around a campfire singing, 'Yo-ho, Rumbleskilstin—'"

"Excuse me?" Della said. *"Rumbleskilstin?"*

The servant repeated it, incorrectly again, saying, "He sang, 'Yo-ho, Rumbleskilstin is my name. Rumbleskilstin, Rumbleskilstin, Rumbleskilstin. The king doesn't know it. The queen doesn't know it. Only I know it, and I'm Rumbleskilstin.'"

"That's quite a song," Della said, trying not to laugh at the picture of the normally dignified Rumpelstiltskin dancing around a campfire, and—after all that—the servant getting the name wrong. Still, Rumpelstiltskin certainly wouldn't complain that it wasn't exactly right. "Well," she agreed, "this is indeed fortunate. You have our gratitude, mine and the king's."

At least Della hoped the king would be grateful.

Rumpelstiltskin appeared in the throne room at the appointed time, but the king was late getting back from an appointment with the royal wigmaker. When the king did come in, laughing and chatting with his companions, he didn't appear nearly as worried as Rumpelstiltskin did.

"We discovered a likely name," Della told the king.

"Good," he said, fluffing his new wig, which was even curlier than his other 150 wigs.

Look at me, Della thought at him furiously. *Look at your daughter.*

But the king looked, instead, at his reflection in the mirror and blew kisses to himself.

Hugging the baby close, Della turned to Rumpelstiltskin, who *was* looking at them. *No one can change straw into gold,* Della thought to herself. *Some things are just straw, and some things are gold, and sometimes you just have to know which is which.*

She walked past the king to put her hand on Rumpelstiltskin's arm, looked up into the young elf's eyes, and said, "Take us with you."

So Rumpelstiltskin put his arm around her and stepped sideways, as always, between the particles.

The king, of course, hired his own messengers to spread the news of what had happened. But as for Rumpelstiltskin and Della, they lived happily ever after. And it was Rumpelstiltskin who chose the name for Della's baby girl. He called her Abigail, which means "a father's joy."

III

The domovoi

Once upon a time, before home security systems and trained guard dogs, if you lived in Russia the way to keep your house safe and happy was to have a domovoi living beneath your basement. Domoviye were—or are: sometimes such things are hard to be certain of—short and hairy, looking something like overstuffed teddy bears, except with longer fur, smaller noses, and very nimble fingers. Shy but gentle hearted, domoviye would use their magical powers however they were needed to keep the people who lived in the houses above them safe and happy. Not every house had a domovoi, but every domovoi had a house. The way to keep a domovoi beneath *your* house and not running away to live beneath your neighbor's basement was to put out a saucer of cream every night, and—once in a while—a plate of sweets.

Now, the biggest house in Russia at that time was the

palace of the king, and the domovoi who lived beneath the palace basement was named Rumpelstiltskin. The king, as his father before him and *his* father before him, enjoyed balls and parties more than politics and running a kingdom, so he and his household were generally happy. And if the people of the land were not happy, nobody in the king's house knew it. The household included many servants who knew all about domoviye, and they all left out cream and sweets for him. As a consequence, Rumpelstiltskin had gotten rather fat and very lazy, though he remained as shy and good natured as ever.

But one day Rumpelstiltskin was awakened from his early evening nap by the sound of someone crying.

Crying? he thought. Someone was *crying* in the house he was supposed to make safe and happy? Rumpelstiltskin had already had his morning nap, and he'd already had his afternoon nap. So he knew he wasn't hearing things from being overtired. He had already had two saucers of cream this evening, so he knew he wasn't hearing things from being weak from hunger. Someone was crying: not laughing, not sniffling with a cold. Crying.

Rumpelstiltskin burrowed up through the floor—the tunnels a domovoi makes are magical and close up after him—and he burrowed through the walls, and he burrowed through the ceilings, all the while following the sounds of the crying.

He ended up in a tower room, filled with sweet-smelling, soft straw. *Wonderful fresh straw for snuggling into and going to sleep in,* Rumpelstiltskin thought. *THAT should make someone happy.*

But the person in the room was *definitely* not happy. The person in the room was a young woman, sitting at a stool pulled up to a spinning wheel, and her eyes were red, and her cheeks tear-streaked. Though she wasn't one of the house's usual occupants, as long as she was here, she was Rumpelstiltskin's responsibility.

So he said, "Don't cry, pretty lady," hoping that by calling her "pretty lady," he would make her happy, even though she was too puffy and slimy with tears and snot to be honestly called pretty. She looked so young—a girl, really, and that gave Rumpelstiltskin an idea. "Don't cry, and Rumpelstiltskin will do a trick for you." He tried to stand on his head, which sometimes in the past had made little children forget their troubles. But he'd gotten so fat he kept tumbling over until finally he gave up and did it propped against the wall. "Ta-dah!" he said, spreading his arms wide.

But even upside down he could see that the girl had

buried her face in her hands, and her shoulders were shaking. If the blood wasn't rushing to his head, he would have heard her crying still.

Rumpelstiltskin scrambled back to right-side up and ran to the girl's knee, which was just about how tall he was. "Don't cry, don't cry," he begged her. "Rumpelstiltskin can make everything right. Tell Rumpelstiltskin your troubles, and he'll make your troubles go away."

The girl didn't even look at him. "You can't," she sobbed.

"Look," Rumpelstiltskin said. "Look." He picked up a handful of straw and tugged at her sleeve. "Look, pretty lady. She what Rumpelstiltskin can do."

She finally looked up.

"Rumpelstiltskin can make your troubles go away like this." He held out the handful of straw and made it disappear, hoping that magic tricks would cheer her up.

"I don't need the straw to *disappear*," the girl wailed. "I need it to turn to gold."

"Gold straw?" Rumpelstiltskin asked. "Rumpelstiltskin doesn't understand."

"The king wants me to spin this straw into gold," the girl said, gesturing to that whole big roomful of straw. She was crying so hard she began to hiccup.

"Ooooh," Rumpelstiltskin said, impressed. "Such a *clever* pretty lady to know how to spin straw into gold." It had taken Rumpelstiltskin a good fifty years to learn how to spin straw into gold.

The girl stamped her foot, coming close to stamping on Rumpelstiltskin. "But I *don't* know how to do it," she told him. "That's the whole point. And the king is going to burn me at the stake in the morning."

That didn't sound happy *or* safe.

Rumpelstiltskin sat down on the floor, close to the girl but far enough away to keep his toes unharmed in case she brought her foot down again. "Tell Rumpelstiltskin," he said. "Tell from the beginning."

The girl wiped her nose on her sleeve. "From the beginning," she said, her voice giving a little quaver, but then she gave a great sniffle and continued more strongly. "My name is Katya."

Rumpelstiltskin jumped to his feet and bowed. "Rumpelstiltskin," he introduced himself.

Katya wiped her nose again and said, obviously not caring *what* his name was, "My father is the miller in the town."

"That must be very interesting," Rumpelstiltskin said encouragingly, sitting down once more.

"Do you want to hear the story or don't you?" Katya demanded, and Rumpelstiltskin, being a clever domovoi, guessed he'd do a better job of making her happy if he listened rather than encouraged. He nodded his furry little head to show how eager he was to listen and not speak.

"Well," Katya continued, "this evening, after work, my father decided to go to the tavern for a drink of vodka, and who else should be there?"

Rumpelstiltskin had to make a quick decision and decided she didn't really want an answer, so he just cocked his head to show he was still eagerly listening.

And, sure enough, Katya continued without waiting for him. "The king. The king was there in our tavern. He'd been riding in his royal carriage and the wheel broke, right in front of the tavern. So he decided to go in and have some vodka."

Rumpelstiltskin began to notice a trend in all this, but he didn't point it out.

Katya said, "So there's my father, and there's the king. My father, of course, has never seen anybody more important than the master of the Millers' Guild, much less been in the same room with the king. So what does my father do?"

Rumpelstiltskin raised his eyebrows to indicate he wondered—but would never ask—*What?*

"My father goes up to the king to offer to buy him some vodka."

Rumpelstiltskin didn't know what reaction Katya wanted so he tried to look impressed and aghast all at once, and—of course—deeply interested.

"So my father buys the king a vodka, and the king buys my father a vodka, and my father buys the king a vodka, and so on and so forth: nobody wants the other to outdo him. So, they're drinking and they're talking, and guess what my father tells the king?"

Rumpelstiltskin smiled to encourage her to go on.

"Well?" Katya snapped. "Aren't you listening? How can you help me if you aren't listening?"

Rumpelstiltskin guessed she wanted an answer this time. "Rumpelstiltskin is listening," he assured her. "Rumpelstiltskin just doesn't know what your father said to the king."

"*He said,*" Katya explained from between clenched teeth as though she was tired of dealing with Rumpelstiltskin, "'My daughter can spin straw into gold.'" She gestured around the room as though to ask how Rumpelstiltskin could possibly have forgotten. "Now why," she asked, "would my father have said such a thing?"

Rumpelstiltskin suspected that maybe all that vodka might have had something to do with it, but then again Rumpelstiltskin preferred saucers of cream.

"And why," Katya asked, her voice rising into a wail again, "would the king ever have believed such a thing?"

The answer was the same as last time, but still Rumpelstiltskin didn't say it.

"And now the king has said," Katya finished, "—in case you weren't listening before—that if I don't spin this straw into gold by morning, he's going to burn me at the stake."

Rumpelstiltskin doubted the king would do such a thing: he'd always seemed such a reasonable man. Rumpelstiltskin said, "In the morning, king will have forgotten all about it. King will drink tea for his headache and say to himself, 'What is all this straw doing in my tower room?' and he will send Katya home to her father, who will be needing tea, too. Rumpelstiltskin will give Katya a good tea for headaches."

Katya brought her foot down so sharply Rumpelstiltskin was glad he had moved his toes. "You're hopeless. The king will burn me at the stake, and you're talking about tea."

Rumpelstiltskin saw that she wouldn't be convinced. She would spend all night fretting and weeping, certain she was to die in the morning. A very unhappy household. The thought made the domovoi shiver. He said, "Rumpelstiltskin will lead Katya out of the castle so she can go home tonight."

"Oh, that's clever!" Katya snapped. "Then tomorrow morning the king can come and get me, and then burn me at the stake in my very own front yard."

"No, no, no," Rumpelstiltskin said. "King would never do that."

"You didn't hear him," Katya sniffed.

Rumpelstiltskin thought and thought. How could he make this girl happy? He said, "King is not here. King will not see if Katya spins straw into gold or if Rumpelstiltskin spins straw into gold. Rumpelstiltskin will spin straw into gold for Katya." *That,* he thought, should cheer her up.

"You know how to spin straw into gold?" Katya demanded.

Rumpelstiltskin nodded.

"And you never told me till now?" She rolled her eyes in exasperation. Then she said, "Here," and she took off a tiny gold ring from her finger. "*If* you can really spin all this straw into gold, I'll give you this ring."

Since Rumpelstiltskin knew how to spin straw into gold, he didn't need a gold ring. In fact, being a domovoi, he didn't need anything but a house to live under, a saucer of cream every night, and—once in a while—a plate of sweets. So he shook his head.

"Don't you try getting more out of me," Katya warned, placing her hand protectively over the thin gold chain around her neck. "I'm offering you the ring: Take it or leave it."

Rumpelstiltskin decided she wouldn't be happy until he took the ring, so he took it.

"Ha!" Katya said, and got up from the stool next to the spinning wheel.

Rumpelstiltskin sat down and began to spin.

Spin and spin and spin, all night long while Katya slept on the straw. *Whir, whir, whir* went the wheel, changing straw to gold. Round, round, round went the spindle as Rumpelstiltskin worked through his late-night nap and missed his third saucer of cream. Till finally by morning—Rumpelstiltskin had to nudge the sleeping Katya off the last of the straw so he could spin that, too—finally he was finished.

There was a loud clattering at the door: someone unlocking it.

Katya jumped to her feet. "Don't let anybody see you," she warned Rumpelstiltskin in a whisper. She began brushing stray tiny pieces of straw from her skirt.

Rumpelstiltskin bowed and burrowed down into the floor, through the ceilings, through the walls, back to his place beneath the lowest basement, feeling the happiness of the household through every bone in his domovoi body. Exhausted but pleased, he settled down for a good morning's sleep.

He was awakened from his early evening nap by the sound of crying. *Someone is not happy,* he thought. It was strange that he had gone for almost a whole year without anybody being unhappy in the house, and now someone was crying for the second night in a row. He followed the sound.

There was Katya again, by a spinning wheel, sitting in an even bigger room than before, surrounded by even more straw than before. The king, Rumpelstiltskin guessed, must have realized that—vodka or no vodka—he had stumbled upon a good thing.

Katya jumped up as soon as she saw him and unclasped her gold necklace. "Here," she said. "I'll give you this if you spin more straw into gold."

Rumpelstiltskin shook his head. He couldn't possibly take her necklace. There was a crow that lived under the eaves of the castle, and Rumpelstiltskin had given him the ring, knowing he liked shiny things. Rumpelstiltskin was about to tell Katya she would spoil the crow by giving him her necklace, but she put the necklace into his hand and closed his fingers around it. "Take it," she insisted angrily. "I don't have anything else."

Since that was the only thing that would make her happy, Rumpelstiltskin nodded his head. Then he sat down and began to spin.

Once more Rumpelstiltskin worked through his late-night nap and his second as well as his third saucer of cream, till finally, just as morning dawned, he finished. There was scuffling outside the door and, as Katya straightened her skirt and fluffed her hair, Rumpelstiltskin bowed and left before he could be asked to. Back beneath the lowest basement, where it was dark and quiet, and at last feeling the happiness in the household, Rumpelstiltskin fell asleep.

And woke up yet again to the sound of crying. It was earliest evening, and he had had *no* saucer of cream at all. But, being a domovoi, he couldn't ignore the sound of unhappiness. It couldn't be Katya again, he thought: not three nights in a row. Surely she had to be happy now. Through the walls and floors and ceilings he burrowed, finding himself at last in a tower room that was bigger yet than the other two, and filled with—somehow he had guessed though he'd told himself *no*—straw.

"You've taken all I have from me," Katya cried.

Rumpelstiltskin wanted to tell her he could get the ring

back from the crow, and the necklace back from the mouse to whom he'd given that. But he didn't have time.

Katya said, "All right, all right. I promise to give you my firstborn child."

Rumpelstiltskin knew this was wrong. A ring can go to a crow, and a necklace can go to a mouse, but the child of those who live above the basement belongs with its own kind.

"No," he said.

"The king has promised that this is the last time," Katya said. "He said that if I spin this straw into gold, he will marry me."

"No," Rumpelstiltskin repeated.

"It's the only thing in the world that will make me happy," Katya said, knowing what a domovoi was.

"No," Rumpelstiltskin said yet again.

Katya covered her ears and began to scream.

It was a terrible sound that would have been annoying to most, but it was heartbreaking to a domovoi, and it went on and on and on until Rumpelstiltskin couldn't take it anymore and he went and sat down at the spinning wheel and began to spin.

Katya is very young, Rumpelstiltskin thought as he spun. *And a little bit foolish. By the time she is married, by the time she has a child, she will have forgotten her promise, and then everybody will be happy.*

And that, Rumpelstiltskin thought, was the end of that.

Happiness filled the house in the following days as the king announced to all that he would marry Katya. Happiness filled the house in the following weeks as there were engagement parties and preparations for the marriage feast, and then the marriage feast itself, and afterward celebration parties. Happiness filled the house in the following months, for the king and Katya both loved eating and drinking and dancing and being the center of attention, so they were well suited to each other and stayed out of the affairs of others. The kingdom rejoiced.

Rumpelstiltskin got fatter and lazier and he basked in contentment even when it was announced that Katya was with child, for Katya was happy, and that meant she had forgotten her promise, and that was fine with Rumpelstiltskin.

And then the baby was born, a handsome boy, which made everyone happier yet.

. . . Until the child's nurse set down a saucer of cream on the floor of the new prince's room, and said, "We are *so* fortunate—here's an extra saucer of cream for the domovoi to thank him for all the luck this family has had," and then

Katya's unhappiness cut through walls and ceilings and floors, straight to Rumpelstiltskin's heart so that he could hear all that was said in the room so high above him.

"No!" Katya cried. "Oh, no, no, no! It cannot be! Send for my husband! *Send for my husband!*"

The king did not have to be sent for; he came running into the room. "Katya, my love! What is it? What's wrong? Has something happened that we'll have to cancel tonight's ball?"

"I promised our child away!" Katya admitted with great racking sobs. "I promised our child away!"

"What?" the king asked. "To whom? Why? I don't understand."

Domoviye are shy creatures. They rarely show themselves, and if they do it's to one person alone, the way Rumpelstiltskin had come to the various rooms Katya had been in.

But there was so much unhappiness, Rumpelstiltskin couldn't help himself. He burrowed through walls, floors, ceilings, to the nursery.

"There!" Katya shouted, her voice and her finger shaking as she pointed at him. "He made me promise our child away in return for showing me how to spin straw into gold for *you.*"

Rumpelstiltskin would have explained that he didn't

want the child, that he could get back the necklace and the ring too, if Katya and the king wanted, but the king didn't give him a chance.

"Vile creature!" the king shouted. "Out! Get out!" He kicked over the saucer of cream, spreading a stream of white over the blue-painted floor.

Domoviye do not stay where they are not wanted. Rumpelstiltskin burrowed down, down, down, straight down, without even caring if the people of the household he passed noticed him, straight to his place beneath the basement, and then sideways, out, out, out from beneath the castle walls, under the yard, until he found himself beneath the basement of the cottage of the family of the goat keeper.

Rumpelstiltskin sniffed the air and found there was contentment in the house. Also a cat, which probably meant saucers of cream. Rumpelstiltskin stayed where he was, rocking miserably backward and forward in the dark.

But there was so much unhappiness coming from the nearby castle, that it washed over even as far as the cottage.

They were afraid, Rumpelstiltskin could tell, afraid that he would come back for the baby.

That night's palace ball centered on the theme Guess the Monster's Name.

"An evil named," the king said, unhappily enough for Rumpelstiltskin, beneath the goat keeper's cottage, to overhear, "is an evil conquered. If we could only name this creature . . ."

Rumpelstiltskin, Rumpelstiltskin thought. He had introduced himself to Katya.

But apparently Katya had only been paying attention to herself, for, weeping, she said she did not know his name.

Rumpelstiltskin took the saucer of cream the goat keeper had set out for the cat and, carrying it carefully, he burrowed into the earth, through the yard, and up through the castle floors, until he found himself in the baby's room.

The nurse was asleep in her chair beside the baby prince's cradle.

Good, Rumpelstiltskin thought. The floor was painted blue, a good background color for showing up cream. Rumpelstiltskin dipped his finger into the saucer he'd carried with him and began tracing letters onto the floor: first an R, then a U . . .

When he was finished, he picked up the saucer and threw it onto the floor to get everyone's attention. The nurse woke up, guards rushed in, and the king and Katya came running in, too.

"He's come to steal our baby!" Katya screeched, though

Rumpelstiltskin wasn't standing anywhere near the baby; he was standing by his name, which he'd written in cream on the blue-painted floor.

"Don't anybody move," the king commanded. "Maybe we can try reasoning with him."

"Why, someone's written something on the floor," one of the guards said, "and he was about to rub it out."

Which was exactly wrong, but at least it got everybody looking at the floor.

"It looks like a name," the nurse said. "It looks like . . ." She was trying to read it upside down and backward. "N . . . I . . . K—Nikolaus?"

"R, said one of the guards, who was clever enough to see which end was up. "Could it be Robert?"

They were all rolling their R's and trying to sound out *Rumpelstiltskin*. As soon as someone—it was Katya, by chance—said something that started with an R and had four syllables, Rumpelstiltskin pulled his hair and gave a cry that he hoped sounded more like frustration than heartfelt relief, and he stamped his foot and burrowed deep, deep into the ground. He could feel the relief of the household wash over him, thinking they had outwitted him and they were safe.

Now he just needed to be safe from them, for they were

too foolish and unreliable to stay happy for long. He burrowed past the goat keeper's cottage, past the outer walls of the town, and kept on burrowing until he reached the house of a little old lady who kept more cats than she could count.

"Some people," Rumpelstiltskin told the cats, "just aren't happy unless they aren't happy."

None of the cats disagreed, so Rumpelstiltskin decided that they were fine and clever cats, and he lived with them for many, many happy years.

IV
papa rumpelstiltskin

Once upon a time, before bread was plastic-wrapped and sold in supermarkets, there lived a miller named Otto and his daughter, Christina.

In the way of most fathers, Otto was proud of his daughter and liked to brag about her. "Christina is a very clever girl," he told people. "Christina is a very sweet girl," he told people. "Christina is a very brave girl," he told people.

One of the things the miller was especially proud of was Christina's talent at spinning. "Christina," he would say, "can take the coarsest, lumpiest wool, and she can spin it into thread as thin as a spider's web." Or sometimes he'd say, "Why, I've seen Christina take flax that's so woody any other spinner would just throw it away, but Christina spins it fine as a cloud." And sometimes, when he was feeling especially proud, he'd say, "That Christina! She could spin straw into gold!"

One day, over the noise of the river turning the wheel that turned the gears that turned the mill wheel that ground grain into flour, Otto and Christina heard the blare of trumpets. Three fine coaches had pulled up in front of the mill, and, walking ahead to announce their arrival, were two satin-dressed servants. Out of the middle coach stepped the lord high chamberlain of the land. He ignored Otto and his daughter, who were rushing outside, trying to make themselves presentable in a hurry by wiping their hands on their work aprons. Instead, the lord high chamberlain went to the first coach, and by the way he bowed, Otto knew immediately that its passenger must be the king.

Otto bowed and Christina curtsied as the king stepped from the coach.

The king took out a lacy handkerchief and waved it lazily in Christina's general direction, because—of course—he was too important to speak to commoners.

In a bored voice, as though he was used to talking to much more interesting people than millers, the lord high chamberlain said, "The king asks: 'Is this the girl who can spin straw into gold?'"

Uh-oh, Otto thought.

Meanwhile, Christina, sounding amazed, asked, "Me?" and then, sounding puzzled, said, "No."

The king pursed his lips disapprovingly.

The lord high chamberlain said, "Don't contradict the king."

Otto cleared his throat.

"But—" Christina started.

The king, however, was waving his handkerchief in the general direction of Otto, and the lord high chamberlain said, "Don't interrupt the king. The king asks: 'Is this the man who says his daughter can spin straw into gold?'"

Christina put her hand on her hip and looked at her father in shocked wonder.

Otto stammered, trying to say, "Well," "Yes," "But," and "I only meant" all at the same time.

Apparently the king heard only the "Yes" part. He waved his handkerchief at Christina again, then at the third coach, then—as though this had soiled the lace—he let the handkerchief drop to the ground and he got back into his own coach.

"The king says," the lord high chamberlain told Christina, "that you are to come with us. You are to spin straw into gold tonight, or tomorrow morning he will have you put to death."

"What?" Otto said.

"What?" Christina said.

The lord high chamberlain took a box of snuff, sniffed a pinch, and repeated, sounding as bored as ever, "The king says: 'You are to come with us. You are to spin straw into gold tonight, or tomorrow morning he will have you put to death.'"

Otto stepped forward to protect his Christina. "This is all a misunderstanding," he started.

"Are you asking," the lord high chamberlain asked him, "for the king to have your daughter put to death *now?*"

"No!" Otto hurriedly placed himself between the lord high chamberlain and Christina. "We'll come with you."

"The coach," the lord high chamberlain sniffed, "is for the girl."

While Otto was helping Christina up into the last coach, he took the opportunity to whisper to her, "This is all my fault. But I'll follow in our wagon, and I'll think of a plan to rescue you."

"Mmmm," said Christina, who, of course, knew her father well. "Do be careful. I'll try to think of something, too."

The lord high chamberlain got back into the middle coach, and Christina leaned out of the window to kiss her father's cheek.

Quickly Otto hitched his horse to the wagon he used to

make deliveries and set off after the coaches. All the while that the coaches drove along the river from the mill through the woods to the castle, Otto thought.

I could bring my wagon beside the coach that holds Christina, and she could squeeze through the window and jump out and into the wagon, he thought.

But surely the king would notice. And he would send soldiers after them. *Perhaps,* Otto thought, *I'd better think some more.*

At the castle, servants lowered the drawbridge that let the three coaches and the miller's wagon cross the river to the castle itself, which stood on an island in the river. Once they were inside, Otto watched as the bridge was raised again, trapping them inside. This ruined the second plan he had devised, which was to wait until night and then sneak out of the castle with his daughter.

He climbed out of his wagon and approached Christina, who was just getting down from the coach. He whispered his third plan to her. "Maybe if we hire a very clever lawyer—"

Christina shook her head. "Lawyers take too long," she pointed out. "By the time a lawyer sets a court date . . ." She shuddered, and Otto did, too. Otto wasn't very good at plans, but he knew what being too late would mean for his daughter. Christina said, "Obviously I don't know how to spin straw into gold. In fact, the only gold we have is the gold necklace that was my mother's before she died."

Otto watched as Christina pulled the chain up over her head. Otto said, "Do you want me to bribe the lord high chamberlain?"

"I doubt this would be enough," Christina said. And, in fact, Otto could see the man approaching, now that servants had helped the king out of his coach and into the castle. Otto did have to admit to himself that there was more gold in the embroidery of the lord high chamberlain's vest pocket than was in the entire necklace Christina held.

"Hurry," Christina whispered to her father. "Take the necklace to a goldsmith and ask him to melt it down and draw it out into gold wire. Maybe the king will be satisfied with that."

"Clever Christina!" Otto cried.

"Shhh," she warned.

Otto lowered his voice. "What about the straw? If you're supposed to have spun it into gold, you'll need to get it out of the room."

Christina spoke quickly, for the lord high chamberlain was only a few steps away. "Place our wagon outside the window," she said. "Once night falls, I will throw the straw out the window into the wagon, then you must drive it away."

"Christina, you are brilliant!" Otto said. He turned to the lord high chamberlain. "My Christina is *so* smart—" he started, but Christina said sternly, "Father. Not now."

"Oh," Otto said, realizing that she didn't want the king's people knowing she was clever enough to outsmart them. "Right," he said. "Never mind."

So Otto didn't say anything when the king's servants came, but silently followed as they led Christina to a room filled with straw.

It was, Otto saw, an incredible amount of straw. Christina didn't point that out. She didn't object that even if all the straw had been wool, and even if she had only to spin it into yarn, there was no way she could have done it all in one night. Instead, she said, "This is a magnificent spinning wheel the king has provided for me, but it's not what I'm used to. I'm sure I could spin much better if my father brought me my own."

Word was sent to the king, who gave his permission, and the miller left on his errand for Christina, knowing that if he did not return in time, the king would have his daughter killed.

Luckily, the goldsmith was able to melt the necklace

and pull it out into fine wire. Otto had him wrap it around a spool, which Otto then fastened to the bottom of Christina's spinning wheel. Placing the spinning wheel into the wagon, he returned to the king's castle.

There, he carried the spinning wheel up the stairs to Christina's lonely room, and—when nobody was looking—pointed to where the spool was set on a nail beneath the seat.

Christina blew him a kiss as the servants told him it was time for him to leave so that she could begin spinning for the king. "Such a brave girl," Otto pointed out to the servants.

But they really weren't interested.

Once darkness fell, Otto drove the wagon so that it was directly beneath the window of the room in which Christina was locked. She began to toss armful after armful of straw out the window. Below her, Otto arranged armful after armful of straw into the wagon.

It was hard work, and it took all night. Just as dawn was breaking, Otto drove the wagon around to the royal stables. "Straw delivery for you," he announced to the stable master, who helped him unload the wagon.

As soon as that was done, Otto raced back to the castle. He was just in time to see a crowd gathered in the hall in front of the room in which Christina was locked. He was just in time to hear the lord high chamberlain proclaim, "The king commands: 'Open the door.'"

A servant opened the door, and the lords and ladies of the court all crowded together, trying to see in. Standing in the center of the doorway, with nobody crowding him, was the king. Standing at the back of the crowd was Otto.

"No straw," Otto could hear various people murmur, as the news spread to the back of the crowd.

Until, finally, someone asked, "But where's the gold?"

Otto saw Christina take a deep breath, then she pulled out from behind her back the spinning wheel spindle. She had wrapped the gold wire from the goldsmith's spool around it.

More appreciative murmurings.

Except from the king. The king motioned with a lace handkerchief at the spindle, then around the room, which was empty save for Christina, the spinning wheel, and one or two stray pieces of broken straw.

"The king wonders," the lord high chamberlain interpreted, "where the rest of the gold is."

Uh-oh! Otto thought.

But his brave Christina didn't look worried. She curtsied. "Apparently your majesty is not familiar with spinning. But if your majesty should ask one of the women who spins, such a woman could tell you that the raw wool—or flax—or straw—is always much bulkier than the finished thread it works down to."

From the court ladies—who of course never did their own spinning but who had seen their maids work—there came a gentle sigh of agreement.

The king was displeased, Otto could tell. He wanted more gold.

To protect his daughter, Otto said, "Christina can do a lot better than this. Just give her more straw."

Christina glared at her father, but it was too late.

The king finally took the spindle from her. He gestured with his handkerchief—Otto had no idea what he could possibly mean—then he turned and walked away, with the lords and ladies trailing behind him.

In the end, only the lord high chamberlain was left, and some servants, and Otto—who hadn't been able to get near while the crowd had been there. Now he held his arms wide, and Christina ran to hug him. "Sorry," Otto told her, "sorry," hoping that his bragging words had caused no harm.

The lord high chamberlain, who'd been busy with his snuff box, finally finished, and he told the servants, "Feed her and let her rest. The king commands that tonight she will spin more straw into gold, or she will pay with her life."

"But," Christina said as the servants took her by the arms and led her down the hall, away from her father. "But . . ."

That evening, before the servants locked Christina into her new prison room—a room that was even bigger than the first and even more full of straw—Otto asked to see her.

"I've brought this pillow," he said. "I forgot to bring it last night for you to sit on." He spoke loudly, because the servants were listening. Then he whispered to her, "Same plan as last night?"

"I only had one necklace," she reminded him.

Otto told her, "I sold all our clothes and furniture. There are two spools of gold wire sewn into the pillow. The wagon is outside this window. Start throwing."

So Christina did.

Otto collected the straw in the wagon and brought it to the stable, to the stable master, who was relieved to receive it, for—he told Otto—there seemed to be a sudden shortage of straw in the last couple of days.

By the time Otto arrived at Christina's room, the servant was just opening the door for the king and his court.

Otto saw Christina immediately hold out the spindle with two spoolsful of gold wire. "Thank you for your kind hospitality," she told the king. "But I've been so lonely for home, I cannot stay a moment longer."

Hardly even glancing at the gold, the king took out his handkerchief and began waving.

Otto sincerely hoped he was saying good-bye.

The lord high chamberlain said, "The king understands your distress. But he says that from now on this is your home. In fact, the king has graciously agreed to marry you tomorrow."

Otto saw the horror with which Christina looked at him.

How could he possibly think she'd want to marry someone who keeps threatening to kill her? Otto wondered. The crowd, however, broke into polite applause.

"Of course," the lord high chamberlain continued, "as queen, you will not only spin straw into gold every day; you will also teach the castle servants how to do so."

He didn't have to add, "Or else." Otto could read it in his eyes. No doubt Christina could, too.

Once again, the king and his court left Christina with

the servants, and—waiting at the edge of the crowd—her father. "I had the feeling you might need this second pillow," he said.

"Oh, Father!" She threw her arms around his neck.

"I thought this might happen," he whispered. "Well, not the marriage part, but the more gold part. So I sold the mill."

"Father!" she gasped. The mill was their livelihood. And after all, they both knew it would gain them only one day.

Unless one of them came up with a better plan.

Otto hoped it would be Christina, because he'd had enough trouble just keeping up with her first plan.

That night the servants locked Christina in the main audience hall—the largest room in the castle. But when Otto drove the wagon around the castle, he saw to his dismay that the room was built out so that it hung over the river that surrounded the castle. In fact, it was directly over the entrance to the little cove where the king's ships were anchored. There was no way Otto could get his wagon out into the deep water.

He saw that Christina had opened the window. In the moonlight they looked at each other hopelessly. Then, because there was nothing else they could do, Christina began throwing the straw into the river. If they were lucky, Otto thought, the current would carry it away.

But they hadn't been lucky yet, and by the earliest morning's light, they could see that Christina had thrown in so much that the straw had mounded up, forming a pile that showed through the surface of the water. As soon as anybody looked, what she had done would be discovered.

There was no time to worry. In the new pillow Otto had brought, there were three spools of gold wire—all that was left of their mill—and Christina went to hurriedly wrap these around a spindle as Otto raced to be at the door when it was opened.

He got there just as the king and his court arrived. Beyond them, he could see that Christina remained sitting at the spinning wheel, the filled spindle on the floor beside her, and she was sobbing loudly.

Otto sincerely hoped she was faking. He hoped she had come up with a new plan, for all he could think was to try to get all their friends and neighbors to sign a petition asking the king to let Christina go, and somehow Otto doubted the king would put off his wedding because the townspeople asked him to.

Seeing Christina's tears, the lord high chamberlain demanded, "What's happened?"

"Someone came during the night," Christina gasped between sobs. "The little man who originally taught me to spin straw into gold. When I first wanted to learn, I agreed that in return I would give him my firstborn son. Now that I am to marry the king, the little man insists he shall have the royal child."

Good plan! Otto thought. The king would never allow such a thing.

The crowd in the doorway cried out in dismay. But Otto saw the king wave his handkerchief airily.

"The king says," the lord high chamberlain said, "he is rich enough and powerful enough to protect against any such person. The king says: The wedding will proceed as planned."

The crowd cheered.

This time Otto didn't have a chance to even speak to his daughter before she was led away.

Do you have a plan, Christina? Otto thought at her.

But of course there was no way for her to answer.

Otto had to come up with his own plan.

By the time Otto got back to the castle that afternoon, the spinning wheel had been removed from the audience hall and the floor had been swept clean. Servants had dressed

Christina in a gown decorated with sparkling gems. They had put a gold and ruby necklace around her neck, a gold and sapphire bracelet on one wrist, a gold and emerald bracelet on the other wrist, and a gold and diamond tiara on her head. Presents, no doubt, from the king. This finery cost much more than the gold she had supposedly spun for the king so far, but the king was counting on her to spin for him every day for the rest of her life.

Golden sunlight poured in through the huge floor-to-ceiling windows that lined the walls. The king was sitting on his throne, looking very regal and not at all forgiving, when Otto flung the door open and strode into the room.

"What's all this?" Otto shouted in as big a voice as he could make.

Without Christina to provide him with a plan, Otto had decided that what he needed was a disguise. Except, of course, he had no money to buy one. So he had rolled his clothes in the fireplace of the mill that had used to be theirs, getting the soot of the previous night's fire all over them till they looked as though they were made of black cloth. He smeared more soot into his hair to make that look black, too, and drew a black moustache on his lip. He was aware that as he moved, he left little billows of blackness behind, but he felt that actually the effect was rather dramatic. No one, he thought, would ever recognize him—not in a hundred years.

The king made a dismissive gesture with his handkerchief.

The lord high chamberlain said, "Christina's father, what is the meaning of this?"

"I am not Christina's father," Otto said. "I don't even know who Christina's father is." *Now what?* He continued, "I . . . might bear a slight resemblance to the man, but in truth I am a dangerous magical creature who knows all sorts of enchantments *besides* the spinning of gold from straw, and I have come to take what is rightfully mine. If you don't hand over my—this girl, I will put a terrible spell on all of you."

He had been worried that he looked so frightening, Christina might not realize she was being rescued. And, indeed, he saw that she had clapped her hand to her forehead and that she was shaking her head.

"Of course you're Christina's father," the lord high chamberlain insisted. "You look like him, you sound like him. You're maybe a tiny bit dirtier than him . . ." Impatiently, he called out, "Guards," and two soldiers started approaching. But they were afraid of him—Otto was sure of it. They were laughing, which must mean they were hysterical with fear. Still, they were between Otto and the door.

Christina took her father by the arm and pulled him toward the window through which she had thrown the straw the previous night. This probably meant she recognized him, but—just to be sure—he whispered to her, "It's me. Your father." He could see her wince as though his words gave her a sudden headache. To the king, Otto said, "This girl's firstborn son has been pledged to me. And if that son is yours, too, then once you are dead I will rule your kingdom through him."

Christina smacked him on the back of the head. She hissed into his ear, "There *is* no baby. And there's not going to be one if we get out of here."

"Right," Otto said. "Ahmm . . ." To delay pursuit, he added, "But guess my name, and the bargain is forfeit." He could feel the wall against his back and Christina's tugging on his arm to get him to step up.

The lord high chamberlain insisted, "You *are* Christina's father."

"That's not a name," Otto pointed out.

The king jumped to his feet and spoke for the first time in Otto's hearing—or Christina's hearing, Otto guessed from her expression. The king shouted, "Is the name Rumpelstiltskin?"

Otto was pleased for the opportunity to say, "That's the stupidest thing I ever heard." And with that Christina leapt out the window, so that she landed on the wet heap of straw that clogged the river. Just beyond, the little rowboat Otto had traded the wagon for bobbed in the water.

"Stop them!" the lord high chamberlain's voice cried as Otto jumped and landed with a wet *plop!* beside his daughter.

Otto and Christina scrambled into the boat. Behind them, arrows hit the water as the king's archers began firing. But already Otto was rowing out of their range. And the king's navy would need hours to clear all that wet straw out of the way of their ships.

"You came up with a plan!" Christina congratulated him.

"It wasn't a very good one," Otto protested modestly as the soot ran off his wet skin and puddled at the bottom of the boat.

"No," Christina said. "You were brilliant."

"Well . . ." Otto said, blushing, "maybe just a little bit brilliant."

"Extraordinarily brilliant," Christina corrected. "You just wait until we dock somewhere. I can't wait to tell people how ingenious you are."

"Perhaps 'ingenious' is a bit much," Otto said. "Once you call someone 'ingenious,' then there's a certain type of person who will be constantly testing and teasing and ready to find fault and make fun . . ."

"Oh, no, no, no," Christina insisted. "Ingenious you are, and ingenious I shall call you. Why, as soon as we land, I must start telling people how you tricked the king of our land."

Now Otto knew that if being called ingenious was risking ridicule, being called a tricker-of-kings was risking getting one's head chopped off. Surely his Christina, who was so clever, was clever enough to know that.

"Hmmm," he said. "I think I see your point."

"Yes?" Christina asked.

"I *am* very proud of you," he said.

"And I appreciate that," she told him.

"But I suppose I could be a little more careful about what I say."

"A little more accurate might help, too," Christina said.

"My Christina," Otto said, practicing, "is clever, sweet, and brave. And her spinning isn't half bad either."

"That's a good start," Christina laughed.

Down the river they floated, away from the castle, through the woods, and past the mill that had been theirs, heading they-didn't-know-where. With the gold and finery the king had given Christina to wear, Otto knew the two of them could start again in a different land.

He just hoped it would be ruled by a wiser king.

V

ms. rumpelstiltskin

Once upon a time, before eyelash curlers and lip liner, there lived a very plain girl by the name of Rumpelstiltskin. Rumpelstiltskin was so plain, the other village children called her things like Toad Face and Hairy Beast. *If only I had but one friend,* Rumpelstiltskin thought, *I would be the best friend that person could ever have.* But the children only wanted to torment her and play tricks on her.

The older Rumpelstiltskin got, the plainer she became, till—by the time she was a young lady—she was no longer plain, she was homely.

If only I had a child, Rumpelstiltskin thought, *a baby boy or girl, I would love that child, and that child would love me, and neither of us would care how the other looked.* But Rumpelstiltskin was so homely, the young women of her village all laughed at her; and the young men would not court her or let her court them.

As Rumpelstiltskin got older and older, she became homelier and homelier—till by the time she was a middle-aged lady she was no longer homely, she was ugly.

Rumpelstiltskin was so ugly, the villagers delighted in saying things like: "Is that Rumpelstiltskin looking out the window, or is one of the melons from her garden reflected in the glass?"

And still Rumpelstiltskin dreamed of a baby to love who would love her in return. But in the meantime she kept to herself, and in the darkness of night she read ancient books of magic, and she learned to do things normal village folk could not do.

And all the while she grew uglier and uglier—but by then people no longer called her names or played tricks on her, for everyone was convinced she was a witch.

One day as Rumpelstiltskin worked in her garden, she could hear the sound of a commotion next door. She pulled a stone out from the wall that separated the two yards and saw that a rich carriage had pulled up to her neighbors' house. This was not unusual, for a miller and his daughter lived next door, and rich households as well as poor needed to have their wheat ground to flour before they could bake. But the miller's daughter was weeping and clutching at the front door of the house, while two men dressed in very fine clothes pulled and tugged at her and finally lifted her into the carriage. And all this while nobody moved to help the poor girl, and in fact her own father stood in the yard as the carriage began to drive away.

"I'm sorry!" the father called out after the carriage. "I'm sorry, Luella! I'll do what I can."

Rumpelstiltskin was very curious about what was going on, but she was no longer on speaking terms with any of the villagers. The only way she could learn what this was all about, she decided, was to follow the carriage.

So she did.

Beyond the fields the carriage went, through the woods, over hills and streams, beyond a whole new set of fields, to a magnificent castle.

Well! Rumpelstiltskin thought, recognizing the winged lion emblem on the banners. *The king.*

But what, she wondered, would the king want with a miller's daughter? Surely the king had his own miller to grind flour.

Hiding behind a tree, Rumpelstiltskin watched as the unfortunate Luella was dragged from the coach and carried over the shoulder of one of the king's men into the castle. What had she done, Rumpelstiltskin wondered, to be arrested by the king and imprisoned in his dungeon?

"Why?" Rumpelstiltskin asked. "*Why* would your father say such a thing?"

"Obviously he wanted to impress the king," Luella said in a what-kind-of-fool-are-you? tone.

"Obviously it worked," Rumpelstiltskin snapped right back at her. "Well, all right, I was just wondering. Best of luck to you." She nodded and started to back out the window.

"Wait!" Luella cried. "Little man!"

"Don't call me that," Rumpelstiltskin said. "I'm not a little man." But she waited.

"Oh!" Luella said. "I'm sorry. Truly." She scrambled to her feet and rushed to Rumpelstiltskin's side. "Can you help me? Can you get me out of here?"

"Can you climb?" Rumpelstiltskin asked.

Luella looked out the window and swayed dizzily. "Ooooh, it's even worse in the dark." Luella sank to her knees, and Rumpelstiltskin *did* feel sorry for her. A bit. "He's going to chop my head off," Luella said softly. "The king. He said if I didn't spin this straw into gold by morning, he'd have my head."

"Nonsense," Rumpelstiltskin said. "That wouldn't get him any gold. Surely it was just a threat."

"Still . . ." Luella's sigh indicated that she fully expected to die.

Rumpelstiltskin sighed, too. This girl was just the kind of beauty who always got everything her way, and it was about time she learned a lesson.

But then Rumpelstiltskin sighed again. Getting one's head chopped off was a pretty drastic lesson.

"All right, all right," she said. "I'll spin the straw into gold for you."

"Oh, can you? Will you?" Luella said, jumping to her feet.

Beautiful girls, Rumpelstiltskin thought, *ALWAYS get their own way.* So she said, "If you pay me."

"Oh, certainly," Luella said. She pulled a ring off her finger, a golden ring of the type that boys sometimes give girls to show their friendship. She probably had a dozen more in a drawer at home.

"Oh, a ring!" Rumpelstiltskin muttered. "How useful." But she guessed the king would not be satisfied with one night's gold. It apparently hadn't occurred to Luella to wonder why he should settle for one room of gold if he could have one every night. *Maybe,* Rumpelstiltskin thought, *maybe this can develop into something that would finally benefit ME.* She pulled up the stool with which Luella had been provided and began spinning.

By dawn, she had spun all the straw into gold.

"Thank you, thank you, lit—" Luella caught herself before she finished saying "little man." Instead she finished, more calmly, "Thank you."

"You're welcome," Rumpelstiltskin said, and she bowed and she left, climbing out the window and down the wall. She scurried across the courtyard before the servants were up and about, and she hid in the woods until nightfall.

Once it was dark, she saw that there was no light in the tower room where Luella had been the night before. The king, Rumpelstiltskin would have been willing to bet, was getting greedy.

Traveling from shadow to shadow, Rumpelstiltskin made her way around the outside of the castle, paying special attention to the high-up windows. Sure enough, she found one, in the south tower, that had a light and from which came the sound of someone crying softly.

Rumpelstiltskin scaled the wall and looked in through the crack in the shutters. There was Luella, in a bigger room filled with more straw than before. If Luella had been watching the night before, she might have picked up some of Rumpelstiltskin's techniques. *But that's just like a beautiful woman,* Rumpelstiltskin thought, *waiting for someone else to do it for her.*

Rumpelstiltskin tapped on the shutter, and—to give her credit—Luella seemed to realize immediately who it had to be. She came over and threw open the shutters. "Oh, it's you, lit—It's you. Thank goodness!" She gave the charming smile which no doubt had melted the hearts of all the village youths.

Rumpelstiltskin only said, "More straw."

Luella gestured to indicate the whole huge room. "As you see." But she was not nearly as upset as she'd been the previous night. She was already counting on being rescued.

"What will you give me," Rumpelstiltskin asked, "to spin *this* straw into gold?"

"This locket?" Luella said. She unfastened the chain from around her neck and held the heart-shaped locket up for Rumpelstiltskin to see.

Rumpelstiltskin opened it and saw a tiny painted portrait of a young man. Luella released the chain so that the locket rested in Rumpelstiltskin's hand.

So once again Rumpelstiltskin spent the night spinning straw into gold, and once again she was finished just before dawn, and Luella thanked her, and Rumpelstiltskin left through the window. And once again she waited.

The third night Rumpelstiltskin found Luella not in a

tower room at all, but in the great ballroom. This time Luella had thought beforehand and had opened the shutter herself, so that Rumpelstiltskin could find her.

When Rumpelstiltskin came in through the window, there was barely enough room to step without tripping over all those bales of straw. Still, she saw that Luella hadn't been crying at all. *Presumptuous,* she thought. But that wasn't it, or at least not all of it.

"The king," Luella said, smugly and proud of herself, "has said he will marry me."

Rumpelstiltskin asked, "And what have *you* said to *the king?*"

Luella had to pause to work this out. "Why, I said yes, of course."

"Of course," Rumpelstiltskin said. "On account of his courting you so sweetly." She glanced around at all that straw and decided that Luella was free to make her own choices. "So you won't be needing me." She started to back up to go out the window.

Luella took hold of her arm. "Oh, but I do. One more time. The king said that if I spun this roomful of straw into gold, he'd have more gold than any man had a right to."

That, Rumpelstiltskin thought, *never stopped anyone from wanting more.* But all she said was, "What will you give me for doing this for you?"

"Whatever you want," Luella said.

"*Whatever I want?*" Rumpelstiltskin repeated, remembering for the first time in years that long-ago dream, the only thing she had ever wanted: a child to love her. She tried to shake the ridiculous notion out of her head.

"Gold," Luella said, "however much of it you want. Tomorrow when I'm named queen-to-be, I can give you however much your heart desires."

"*Tomorrow,*" Rumpelstiltskin echoed.

"Well, yes," Luella said with a slight hint of exasperation creeping into her tone. "I have nothing to give you tonight, but tomorrow when the king announces I am to be wed—"

"I," Rumpelstiltskin interrupted, shaking her head, "I don't want your gold, you silly girl. If I can spin straw into gold, what need have I of gold?"

"Well, you took the ring and the locket," Luella said peevishly. "All right, then, pick something besides gold. Gems, clothes, horses." She was getting nowhere. "Servants, lands, a title."

The more she talked, the more Rumpelstiltskin got aggravated with her. *I should never have helped her at all,* she thought. *Spoiled thing that she is. Of course the king will* marry her. *He'll probably even be satisfied with the gold that he has, if he has her, too. They'll live in this castle, with servants to wait on them, and the people of the kingdom to love them, and she'll have dozens of babies, all as pretty and empty-headed as she is.*

Luella stamped her foot. "Well, what do you want, you horrid little man?" she demanded.

Rumpelstiltskin had to fight herself to keep from grabbing Luella and shaking her. "I am *not* a little man," she shouted. "And what I want . . ." *Oh, go ahead, say it.* "What I want is your firstborn child." She couldn't believe the words had come out of her.

Luella gave a hoot of disbelief or protest.

"I mean the child no harm," Rumpelstiltskin said. "And you're young, you're healthy. What's to stop you from having a score of children?"

"You can't be serious," Luella said.

Rumpelstiltskin shrugged. "How serious was the king when he said you must spin or die?"

Luella looked at all that straw.

"You won't have *any* children if you don't give him that gold," Rumpelstiltskin told her.

"All right, all right," Luella said. "First children are always brats, anyway."

So Rumpelstiltskin spun.

‧ ◆ ‧

Whatever Luella told the king, within a month they were married, and within a year the kingdom was celebrating the birth of the royal couple's first child: a baby girl.

Rumpelstiltskin heard no rumors about herself, but she knew that the promise Luella had made to her was one that not even Luella could forget.

One day, after the baby's birth but before its christening, Rumpelstiltskin returned to the castle. That night, while the king was in the great hall celebrating with his lords and barons, Rumpelstiltskin climbed up the castle wall to the room in the eastern tower that, she had learned, was the nursery.

The night was warm and the shutters were open. How could Luella be so careless, so unaware of her danger? Rumpelstiltskin looked in and saw the young mother sitting in a chair, rocking her baby.

Rumpelstiltskin leapt down into the room.

Luella almost dropped the baby, she stood up so quickly. "You!" she cried. "I'd hoped you'd died."

Which at least was an honest reaction, if not a nice one.

Rumpelstiltskin looked down at herself, checking her hands—backs and palms—before looking up at Luella and answering, "Apparently not." Then she said, "I've come for the child you promised me."

"No!" Luella cried. "You can't have her. I've told my husband all about how you came and spun the gold for me. He doesn't care. He's satisfied with the gold he has, and now he loves me, and he would not give me up for anything."

"Lucky you," Rumpelstiltskin said. "But that's neither here nor there. You promised the child in return for my doing a task, and the task was done." Her arms ached with longing to hold the sweetly cooing baby, whose hands flailed about helplessly. *I would be a better mother than you,* she thought.

"Please," Luella wailed, "spare my baby." She fell to her knees. "I beg you. The king and I will reward you in whatever way you ask."

"I ask," Rumpelstiltskin said, "for the baby."

"Why do you want the life of my baby?" Luella sobbed.

"I don't want her life," Rumpelstiltskin assured her. "I mean the child no harm. I want to raise her, as a daughter." She held her arms out for the child, but still she was surprised, unpleasantly so. She wouldn't have thought that Luella was capable of such strong feelings for the child.

"Please, please, please," Luella begged, weeping. "I was so afraid before that I was willing to agree to anything you said. But now I'm even more afraid, on my child's behalf. Please give me another chance to make a different bargain."

Rumpelstiltskin's head was spinning with the mother's tears, and then the door opened and the king walked in.

His face went from jovial to terror stricken as he saw Rumpelstiltskin. "Oh, no!" he cried. "It's the ugly little man you told me about!"

But before Rumpelstiltskin could protest that she wasn't a man, Luella gave a warning hiss. "No, no," she warned her husband, "he doesn't like to be called little."

"Sorry," the king said, so desperate Rumpelstiltskin felt pity for him. "Sorry. Please, please, take anything but our child. Take me, instead."

"Where was that offer thirty years ago?" Rumpelstiltskin muttered. Still, her heart had softened, and she said, "I will give you one more chance."

"Oh, good!" Luella said. Then, very clearly, very distinctly, she said, "I *do not* want you to spin more straw into gold." Triumphantly she added, "There!"

"That's not the chance I meant," Rumpelstiltskin said. "I will pose a riddle. Answer correctly, and I'll let you keep the child." She paused to consider, because she didn't want them to win. What riddle could they never guess? She studied the king and the queen—two self-absorbed people who didn't even look at her closely enough to realize she wasn't a man. She felt her lips twitch in a smile. "What," she asked, "is my name?"

Luella and the king looked at each other in desperate confusion. "How many guesses do we get?" the king asked.

Rumpelstiltskin smacked her forehead with the palm of her hand, but said, "Five guesses."

"Uhm, could it be George?" Luella asked. "Or Stanislaus?"

"Bubba?" the king asked. "Skippy?"

But just then the door flew open and in walked the miller, Luella's father. "Where is that beautiful new granddaughter of mine?" he asked in a cheery voice. Then his eyes went from his daughter, holding the baby, to the king, standing next to her—both looking frantic—to Rumpelstiltskin.

The miller hastily held up his fingers in the sign meant to stop the evil eye. "It's our old neighbor, the witch Rumpelstiltskin!" he cried.

In that self-satisfied tone that only those who are used to being positive of themselves can achieve, Luella shouted, "Is your name Rumpelstiltskin?"

Rumpelstiltskin stamped her foot, infuriated that her

own soft heart had lost her what she most desired. With a cry that was part pain and part fury, she jumped out the window, practically skimming over the surface of the stones that formed the tower.

She went back to her home, whose only joy was her garden, and she never again returned to the castle, determined to raise vegetables rather than children. Still, years later she tried once again to steal a child from parents who struck her as being unfit. They were the couple who lived on the other side of her yard, a couple with an unwholesome appetite for the greens she grew in her garden. She actually ended up raising that child for a while, though in the end things didn't work out there either. But that's a different story.

VI

as good as gold

Once upon a time, before movie stars or rock singers or professional athletes, the people everybody most wanted to meet were kings and queens.

In one particular land there was a king named Gregory. King Gregory was young and handsome and known to be kind, and he was also unmarried—all of which made him very popular with young ladies. But King Gregory's kingdom was being threatened by greedy King Norvin to the west, so Gregory decided he needed to get in touch with his people to make sure they would never choose Norvin over him. Gregory took to getting out of his royal carriage as he traveled through the countryside, and he would walk alongside it, talking to the villagers or farmers he met along the way.

One day as Gregory was passing through a small town, he stopped to watch a blacksmith at his forge. "You do excellent work," Gregory told him. "You're a credit to your craft."

"Thank you, sire," the blacksmith said, pausing only to wipe the sweat from his forehead.

"What about me?" asked a voice from the group that had gathered to watch the king watch the blacksmith. A short man in a long apron stepped forward and announced, "I'm the town's only miller. I think I can honestly say that I keep the town in breads and cakes."

"We passed your fine mill on the way in," Gregory told him enthusiastically. "An admirable place. A praiseworthy establishment. This community is lucky to have you." King Gregory shook the man's hand, then turned back to watch the smith hammer the heated metal to a smooth thin surface.

But the miller pushed his way to the front of the onlookers and tugged on the king's sleeve, demanding his attention. "It's hard work, milling," he said. "Much more complicated than people might think."

"I'm certain it is," Gregory agreed.

"It's one of those things that only *looks* easy to do, but there's all sorts of considerations: the humidity—you wouldn't believe how much the weather affects my work—and the quality of the grain and whether it's early in the season or late, and the weight of the stone, and—"

Gregory shook the man's hand again. "It's incredible that the works gets done at all." He managed to slip his hand out of the miller's grasp. Smiling to the towns-people, he made his way out the door and across the street to where his carriage waited.

The miller followed him. "Of course," he said, "I have my daughter to help me. And a fine daughter she is."

"Well, then, you're both fortunate," Gregory said pleas-antly. The royal footman got down from his perch to help the king into the carriage.

"My daughter," the miller continued, "her name is Car-leen, she's a beautiful girl. *Beautiful.* I think I can honestly say she's the most beautiful girl in the country."

People were always trying to arrange for the king to meet their daughters—who were always the most beauti-ful girl in the country. But Gregory only said, without sarcasm, "Is she?" and settled into his seat.

But the day being fine, the window was open, and the miller leaned in. "I swear," he said. He spoke each word separately and distinctly: "*The. Most. Beautiful.* She would make an excellent wife for *any* man."

Gregory didn't point out that he was looking for more in a wife than beauty. He just smiled politely and gestured for the driver to start.

The miller walked alongside the carriage. "And she isn't

just beautiful," the miller continued, as though he'd read the king's mind. "She's a good girl. And smart. And talented."

"She sounds a credit to her parents and her community," Gregory said. He rapped his knuckles on the front wall of the carriage—a signal to the driver to speed up.

The miller trotted to keep up. "Why, she can sing," he said, "sweet as a nightingale." He was beginning to pant from his attempt to match the pace of the horses. "She weaves cloth of colors that don't even have names yet." As the miller finally began to fall behind, Gregory could no longer see his face, but only his hand clutching the window frame. The miller spoke louder and faster. "And the clothes she sews make the fat look thin, the old look young, the ugly look beautiful." He finally let go of the window. "Not that *she* needs help to look beautiful," he called after the carriage. "I think I can honestly say *that*. She's as good as gold."

Gregory waved out the window.

"In fact," the miller shouted as the carriage made its way up the hill, "she can spin straw into gold."

"That must come in very handy for you," Gregory said. "I'd love to meet her some day." He hoped that the laughter didn't come through in his voice, because he didn't want to hurt the miller's feelings.

He didn't realize that hurting the miller's feelings was the least of his worries.

The following night, just as the castle household was getting ready to settle down for bed, there was a loud commotion at the front gate.

King Gregory went outside to a spot that overlooked the gate. He could see that it was not greedy King Norvin's army come to demand tribute, but apparently only one person, wrapped in a threadbare traveling cloak, banging on the heavy oak door. "What is it?" Gregory asked the captain of the guard. "What's the trouble?"

"It's a young woman, sire, demanding entrance. I told her to come back tomorrow morning, but she says you invited her here. She says she's later than expected and you'll be frantic and that if I don't let her in, once you find out I kept her waiting, you'll have my head chopped off." The captain shrugged apologetically, for it was not Gregory's way to threaten to chop off people's heads.

"I invited her?" Gregory repeated, wondering if he had forgotten some social engagement with a neighboring princess.

"Her name," the captain said, "is Carleen of the town of Roxburough—Carleen the miller's daughter, she says."

Gregory remembered the miller. He sighed in exasperation that the annoying man had sent his poor daughter all the way here for nothing. And apparently on foot. But he couldn't just tell her that; he couldn't say: "Walk on back home even though it's the middle of the night. Your father was wrong. I *don't* want to meet you."

Instead he leaned over the wall and called to the porter at the door, "Let her in. See that she has a comfortable room for the night and that she's given something warm to eat."

Carleen the miller's daughter looked up at the sound of his voice. "Thank you, Your Highness," she called.

She wasn't singing, so maybe it wasn't fair to judge, but even so, Gregory thought she sounded very unlike a nightingale. From this distance, it was difficult to tell much of what she looked like either, except that she was waving. Gregory waved back and turned to leave.

"Yoo-hoo! Your Highness!" Carleen's voice called.

Gregory returned to the wall.

"Don't forget the spinning wheel."

"Excuse me?" Gregory said.

Carleen put her hand on her hip and said, "Well, *duh*. First you expect me to spin straw into gold, then you expect me to do it without a spinning wheel?"

"But I don't—" Gregory started.

"Well, *duh*," Carleen repeated with even more scorn in her voice.

Gregory told the captain, "Get her whatever she needs."

"Yes, sire," the captain said.

"Good night, Your Highness," Carleen called up to him. "Don't you worry about me, walking all yesterday afternoon, then sleeping out in the woods, then walking all day today. I'll stay up all night spinning that straw into gold for you. Don't you give me a second thought."

"Good night, then," Gregory called to her.

He sincerely hoped she'd be gone in the morning.

But in the morning as he was eating his breakfast, he could hear voices raised down the hall, from the wing of the castle where the guests' rooms were. He already had a good guess what that was all about when one of the serving women came in and said, "Excuse me, sire, but it's . . . uhm, your visitor. She says that if you're going to threaten to chop her head off unless she spins straw into gold so that she has to stay up all night spinning, the least you could do is come in the morning to look at the gold."

Carleen seemed, Gregory thought as he followed the servant, to have chopping off heads on the mind.

"Well, there you are," Carleen said when he walked into the room that had been set up for her. It was a comfortable room with a big bed, and thick rugs on the floors to keep feet warm, and tapestries on the walls to keep drafts out. It also had a big spinning wheel in the middle of the floor. "Ta-dah!" Carleen cried triumphantly, and from behind her back she pulled a little golden knob.

"What's this?" Gregory asked.

"*Duh*," Carleen said in that infuriating way of hers. "Well, it sure isn't straw." She *was* pretty—not the most beautiful girl in the country, but pretty. Except, of course, when she stood with her hand on her hip, rolling her eyes and saying "*Duh*."

"I don't understand," Gregory said.

"I spun straw into gold last night. This is the gold."

"There was straw in here last night?" Gregory asked, for straw wasn't normally part of the castle's decor.

The servant woman said, "Yes, she asked for a bale of straw to be sent up, and it was."

"And," Gregory said slowly, noticing that the tapestries on the walls were all lumpy, and that there were little bits of straw on the floor beneath those lumps, "you spun that straw"—Carleen nodded enthusiastically—"into . . . this little knobby thing that looks . . . "—he didn't point to the dresser that was missing a handle—"something like a . . . furniture handle?"

"Yes," Carleen said.

"Well," Gregory said, unwilling to call her a liar. "That *is* a very clever trick. And I want to thank you—and your father—for showing me, and I hope you have a good trip home." He hurriedly added, before she could think of sore feet as an excuse, "You can even use one of the royal carriages. Won't that impress your neighbors?"

"But," Carleen said as he turned to leave, "but it's raining."

"The carriage is covered," Gregory told her.

"But the road will be so muddy, and everybody will be inside, and they won't see the carriage, and nobody will believe me when I tell them I rode in it, and I traveled so hard to get here . . ." Carleen looked so sad, Gregory felt sorry for her.

With a sigh he said, "You may stay another day."

"Thank you, Your Highness!" she said. But as he turned to go, she called after him, "But, Your Highness!"

When he turned back—and he did manage to do it without sighing—she indicated her dress, which was clean and tidy, though nothing elegant, and she said, "Of course, I wouldn't dare leave my room, for shame of my simple peasant's clothes."

If she didn't leave her room, Gregory could be certain he wouldn't run into her, but it hardly seemed fair to invite her to stay, then not let her see the sights. He said to the serving woman, "Find our guest a suitable gown."

"Thank you, Your Highness," Carleen said, curtsying just as the servant had done.

For the rest of the day, every time Gregory looked up, there was Carleen—walking as though she just happened to be passing through the room he was in, or peeking in the doorway to wave at him, or turning her chair at dinner so that she could watch him eat. And it rained all day, so there wasn't even the chance for him to try to lose her in the gardens. Not only that, but each time she saw him look her way, she would give a little jump as though *she* had just happened to notice *him*, after which she would give an energetic wave.

This must be what a rabbit feels like, he thought, *when it's being stalked by a wolf.*

But then he told himself not to worry about her. What he needed to worry about was King Norvin, who was so greedy he wanted to add King Gregory's lands to his own. *That,* he told himself, was a much more serious problem than the miller's daughter. Besides, tomorrow she would be gone.

The following morning at breakfast, Gregory once more heard a commotion from the direction of the guest rooms. When he stepped out into the hall to investigate, one of the serving women came bearing a message from Carleen. The message was: "I'm waiting." Gregory could imagine the impatient tapping of her foot.

"Waiting?" Gregory asked the servant.

"For you to see the straw she's spun into gold," the servant said, all the while looking at a spot three inches above the king's head rather than face him directly.

"Of course," Gregory said with a sigh. "But while I'm seeing to our guest, please notify the grooms to ready the royal carriage so that she may return to her own home."

The servant shuffled her feet.

"What?" Gregory asked. "What's wrong?"

"The captain of the guard came in earlier, sire," the woman said, "bringing news that the rain has washed out the bridge to the town of Roxburough."

"Tell the captain of the guard," Gregory said, "to get that bridge fixed as quickly as possible." But meanwhile he went to Carleen's room.

"Well!" Carleen said, jumping to her feet when he came in. "A bit of a slug-a-bed, aren't we?" She smiled brightly, evidently being one of those people who believe you can say anything if you say it with a smile and pass it off as a joke. "Good thing you were born to be king and didn't have to work to get the job."

Gregory only said mildly, "Good morning."

"I spun this for you," Carleen said, handing him a golden doorknob. "Now you don't have to chop my head off."

Gregory could see that the door to the room was missing its inside knob. He could also see that the drawers in the various chests and dressers weren't closed all the way because they were so stuffed with straw that bits were dangling from the corners. He didn't point any of that out. He said, "Really, Lady Miller's Daughter—"

"Call me Carleen," she told him with a wink.

"You don't need to spin—"

"No, no!" she insisted, holding her hands up as though to stop him. "I understand about kings and gold."

"And I never said anything about—"

She shuddered and covered her ears. "Don't even say it! My head hurts just thinking about it!"

"Well," Gregory said, seeing he was getting nowhere, "thank you for the gold." He looked at the doorknob in his hand and hoped that the bridge could be repaired before there weren't any more fixtures left in the castle.

Throughout the day, Carleen once again always seemed underfoot, waving and blowing kisses every time Gregory glanced in her direction. She began to order the servants around, and made suggestions about the way the rooms were decorated and how things should be done, and dropped hints that she would be very good at running the country.

Gregory suspected he wasn't the only one to be relieved when the captain of the guard sent word that the bridge should be fixed and ready for traffic in the morning.

In the morning, Gregory asked for breakfast in bed because the royal bedchamber was far enough away from the guest rooms that he knew he couldn't hear Carleen, no matter how loud a fuss she made. He was seriously considering staying in his room until she was safely on her way home.

But as he was eating his poached eggs, a servant knocked at the door and said, "Sire, the miller's daughter requests you to come see the straw she has spun into gold."

"Again?" Gregory asked. *Surely,* he thought, *a king has more important things to do than entertain a miller's daughter.* But he went.

Right away Gregory noticed that the bed was mounded

high and lumpy, with straw showing from under the covers. Carleen was wearing the same dress the servants had provided her with, but the long row of golden buttons was gone, and today the gown was held closed by laces. There was a bit of straw showing between the laces, too.

"I spun these for you," Carleen said, holding out to him—surprise!—gold that had apparently been spun to look like buttons.

"Well, thank you," Gregory said, accepting the buttons from her. "Now, much as I hate to say good-bye—"

Carleen burst into tears. "Don't abandon me!" she cried. "The little man will get me and my baby!"

"What little man?" Gregory asked, surprised by this new development. "What baby?"

"The little man who taught me how to spin straw into gold. For some reason he wants me to marry the king." Then—she obviously had no confidence in his ability to reason—she added, "That would be you. He insisted on it. He said if I didn't marry you, he would come and get me. And if I ever tried to marry someone else, he would come and get my baby. So, you see, it's all your fault. And if you don't marry me, my baby and I are both doomed. And people will talk badly about you forevermore."

"And why would this little man want us to be married?" Gregory asked.

"Well, how should I know?" Carleen demanded. "That's just the way some of these little magical creatures are—making stupid rules normal people can't understand. *Duh!* I'd think a king would know about things like that."

How, King Gregory asked himself, *am I ever going to get rid of this awful girl?*

"Now, I don't believe in long engagements," Carleen said, "but don't you worry your little head about getting everything done in time because—just by chance—I've always dreamed of a big wedding,. so I *do* have everything written out, exactly the way I want it, and with just a little bit of urging I'm sure your servants—"

Gregory wasn't paying attention to the droning voice. His concentration had been caught by movement on that part of the front lawn he could see through the window. It could only be the captain of the guard, but he was coated from head to foot with thick mud from working on the bridge repairs all night. He looked, Gregory thought, barely human—like a primeval earth creature. By the way the officer waved jauntily as he approached the castle, the king deduced he must have succeeded in getting the bridge back into working order. Gregory interrupted Carleen. "This little man who threatened you," he said, "he might be the same creature we've heard legends about for as long as this castle has stood here."

"Oh, yes?" Carleen said, obviously relieved that the king didn't require convincing. "Probably."

"Kind of a . . . brown . . . muddy-looking fellow?"

"That's him," Carleen agreed readily.

"Fear not," Gregory told her. "I know how to get rid of him."

"Oh," Carleen said, "I don't think—"

"All we have to do is name his secret name." He leaned forward and added as though sharing a secret, "That's another of those silly rules of magic you were just talking about." Then, before Carleen could complain or object, Gregory said, "Look! That must be him, come to inform me of your bargain." He cranked open the window and called out to the captain of the guard, "Man! Little man!"

The captain of the guard stopped, found the window at which the king was standing, and bowed.

"I will now guess your name," Gregory told him.

The captain of the guard did not point out that, after all the years he had been captain of the guard, the king should already know his name.

"Is it," Gregory asked, "Seymour?"

"No, sire," the captain of the guard answered hesitantly, sounding puzzled.

"Is it Dudley?"

"No, sire."

"Then," Gregory said triumphantly, "could it, by chance, be Rumpelstiltskin?"

"Yes, sire," the captain of the guard answered, by now sounding very puzzled indeed.

"Ha!" Gregory said. "In that case you may go on your way, if you promise to leave alone any child this young lady may ever have."

Captain Rumpelstiltskin, who was married and had more than enough children of his own, held his arms out, dripping little globs of mud. "Certainly, sire," he said, sounding entirely befuddled. "If that is your wish, Your Highness." And he headed off toward the bathhouse.

"See," Gregory told Carleen, "nothing to worry about."

The miller's daughter stamped her foot but had no answer.

Then, knowing he was taking a terrible chance, Gregory said, "But, even though the danger is now gone, would you still be willing to marry me?"

Carleen still had her face screwed up into a disappointed scowl. "What?" she snapped. Then his words must have sunk in. She wiped the sulky look off her face. "Oh," she said. "Yes. Yes, that would be very nice."

Gregory bowed and kissed her hand. "Then I will leave the arrangements to you, my precious. Just be sure you invite King Norvin to the festivities. He is our neighbor to the west, and he is very, very, *very* wealthy. We certainly don't want to slight him."

"Certainly not," Carleen said. Then she asked, "Very wealthy?" She smiled tightly. "How nice for him. Though surely he is not so wealthy as you, my sweet?"

Gregory made an airy gesture of dismissal. "Oh, very much more so," he said. "I am doubly fortunate to have found you because, in truth, this kingdom is rather poor, and your being able to spin straw into gold will come in very handy."

"I . . ." Carleen said, "hadn't realized you'd intended me to keep on spinning straw into gold after we were married. I assumed, as queen, I'd have other important duties."

Gregory said, "Well, of course King Norvin's wife—if he had a wife, which, naturally, he doesn't—King Norvin's wife could concentrate on more frivolous queenly duties such as hosting parties and arranging charity balls and socializing with the nobles, but naturally you won't have time for that lesser kind of responsibility." Gregory smiled encouragingly and added, "Though I'll certainly do my best to see that you have a day off from spinning every once in a while, say on your birthday, maybe, or Christmas." He frowned as though deep in thought. "Well, maybe not *every* Christmas." He kissed her hand once again and said, "So I thank you for your generous offer to help out my kingdom, and you can go ahead now and start the wedding arrangements, if you think you have time."

Carleen was fanning herself with her hand. "Certainly," she said, "certainly. The first thing I need to do is see about getting the invitations, but I'll need to borrow the royal carriage to go to town to order them."

"Of course," Gregory said. "Take as long as you like to choose just the right ones. There will be plenty of time for spinning straw into gold after we're married."

"Yes," Carleen said. "I can see that."

She seemed in an incredible hurry to get started, so Gregory didn't delay her.

But the funny thing was that she never came back from that shopping trip.

The footman and the driver went into the printer's shop looking for her after she'd been gone for more than an hour, but the printer said she'd gone out the back door, and she was last seen heading off toward the west.

By coincidence, within a month King Gregory was invited to the wedding of King Norvin, who was marrying—according to the invitation—a foreign princess by the name of Carleen.

"I'm so sorry matters of state prevent me from attending," Gregory wrote to the happy couple. But as a wedding gift he sent a golden handle, a golden doorknob, and ten golden buttons.